THE PERFECT AFFAIR

THE PERFECT LOOK (Book #6)
THE PERFECT AFFAIR (Book #7)
THE PERFECT ALIBI (Book #8)
THE PERFECT NEIGHBOR (Book #9)

CHLOE FINE PSYCHOLOGICAL SUSPENSE SERIES
NEXT DOOR (Book #1)
A NEIGHBOR'S LIE (Book #2)
CUL DE SAC (Book #3)
SILENT NEIGHBOR (Book #4)
HOMECOMING (Book #5)
TINTED WINDOWS (Book #6)

KATE WISE MYSTERY SERIES
IF SHE KNEW (Book #1)
IF SHE SAW (Book #2)
IF SHE RAN (Book #3)
IF SHE HID (Book #4)
IF SHE FLED (Book #5)
IF SHE FEARED (Book #6)
IF SHE HEARD (Book #7)

THE MAKING OF RILEY PAIGE SERIES
WATCHING (Book #1)
WAITING (Book #2)
LURING (Book #3)
TAKING (Book #4)
STALKING (Book #5)
KILLING (Book #6)

RILEY PAIGE MYSTERY SERIES
ONCE GONE (Book #1)
ONCE TAKEN (Book #2)
ONCE CRAVED (Book #3)
ONCE LURED (Book #4)

ONCE HUNTED (Book #5)
ONCE PINED (Book #6)
ONCE FORSAKEN (Book #7)
ONCE COLD (Book #8)
ONCE STALKED (Book #9)
ONCE LOST (Book #10)
ONCE BURIED (Book #11)
ONCE BOUND (Book #12)
ONCE TRAPPED (Book #13)
ONCE DORMANT (Book #14)
ONCE SHUNNED (Book #15)
ONCE MISSED (Book #16)
ONCE CHOSEN (Book #17)

MACKENZIE WHITE MYSTERY SERIES

BEFORE HE KILLS (Book #1)
BEFORE HE SEES (Book #2)
BEFORE HE COVETS (Book #3)
BEFORE HE TAKES (Book #4)
BEFORE HE NEEDS (Book #5)
BEFORE HE FEELS (Book #6)
BEFORE HE SINS (Book #7)
BEFORE HE HUNTS (Book #8)
BEFORE HE PREYS (Book #9)
BEFORE HE LONGS (Book #10)
BEFORE HE LAPSES (Book #11)
BEFORE HE ENVIES (Book #12)
BEFORE HE STALKS (Book #13)
BEFORE HE HARMS (Book #14)

AVERY BLACK MYSTERY SERIES

CAUSE TO KILL (Book #1)
CAUSE TO RUN (Book #2)
CAUSE TO HIDE (Book #3)
CAUSE TO FEAR (Book #4)

THE PERFECT AFFAIR

(A Jessie Hunt Psychological Suspense Thriller—Book Seven)

BLAKE PIERCE

BLAKE PIERCE

Blake Pierce is author of the bestselling RILEY PAGE mystery series, which includes fifteen books (and counting). Blake Pierce is also the author of the MACKENZIE WHITE mystery series, comprising thirteen books (and counting); of the AVERY BLACK mystery series, comprising six books; of the KERI LOCKE mystery series, comprising five books; of the MAKING OF RILEY PAIGE mystery series, comprising four books (and counting); of the KATE WISE mystery series, comprising six books (and counting); of the CHLOE FINE psychological suspense mystery, comprising five books (and counting); and of the JESSE HUNT psychological suspense thriller series, comprising seven books (and counting).

ONCE GONE (a Riley Paige Mystery—Book #1), BEFORE HE KILLS (A Mackenzie White Mystery—Book I), CAUSE TO KILL (An Avery Black Mystery—Book I), A TRACE OF DEATH (A Keri Locke Mystery—Book I), WATCHING (The Making of Riley Paige—Book I), NEXT DOOR (A Chloe Fine Psychological Suspense Mystery—Book I), THE PERFECT WIFE (A Jessie Hunt Psychological Suspense Thriller—Book One), and IF SHE KNEW (A Kate Wise Mystery—Book I) are each available as a free download on Amazon!

An avid reader and lifelong fan of the mystery and thriller genres, Blake loves to hear from you, so please feel free to visit www.blakepierceauthor.com to learn more and stay in touch.

TABLE OF CONTENTS

CHAPTER ONE

Shots rang out, startling Jessie from her sleep.

Half-awake, she rolled out of bed, grabbed her gun off the side table, and scurried over to the bedroom door. The shots sounded like they had come from the living room. She glanced at the clock: 1:08 a.m.

She set aside how someone could have breached her apartment building's tight security measures to focus on the task at hand. There was a threat on the other side of that door. Not only was she in danger but so was Hannah, who slept in the extra bedroom on the other side of the living room.

Jessie took a long, slow, deep breath before opening the door and peering out. She saw a dim glow in the room before a second round of gunfire made her retrench behind the wall. Had the attacker seen her? She was just preparing to crawl into the living room when she heard a voice.

"You're surrounded, Johnny. Come out with your hands up," a stern male voice instructed.

Suddenly a foreboding musical score kicked in.

"You'll never take me alive!" shouted someone with a distinctly gangster-ish accent.

Jessie allowed herself to breathe normally for the first time in thirty seconds. Lowering her gun, she stood up and stepped into the living room, where she could see the television was on, airing some old black-and-white crime movie.

She grabbed the remote from the coffee table and turned off the TV. Her heart was still pounding as she made her away across the living room, dodging the clothes, shoes, and magazines on the floor, until she got to the open door of Hannah's bedroom.

She poked her head in, where she saw her seventeen-year-old half-sister, Hannah Dorsey, curled up asleep on the bed. The girl had kicked off the covers and was hugging herself as she shivered slightly.

Jessie tiptoed over, grabbed the comforter, and gently draped it back over Hannah, who was mumbling to herself unintelligibly. The criminal profiler stood over her, trying to discern any words. But after a few seconds, she decided it was fruitless and gave up.

She tiptoed back to the doorway, gave one glance back, and then shut the door. She sighed deeply. Despite her repeated pleas not to, this was the third time in the last week that Hannah had left the television on before going to bed. Luckily, it was the first time Jessie had been woken up by the sound of gunfire coming from it.

Part of her wanted to shake the girl awake and drag her out to turn the thing off herself. But, as she'd recently learned from the online parenting newsletter she now subscribed to, teenagers apparently needed lots of extra sleep for their growing minds and bodies. Besides, interrupting Hannah's slumber to prove a point would backfire on her tomorrow in an extra helping of sullenness.

As she crossed the living room to go back to bed, she wondered where the online newsletter was that talked about how almost-thirty-year-old female professionals also needed decent sleep every now and then. She was just smiling to herself when she tripped on a shoe Hannah had left in the middle of the room and stumbled to the floor, slamming her left knee on the hardwood.

She forced herself to stifle the curse word she wanted to yell. Instead she groaned silently as she pulled herself up and limped back to bed. With her knee aching, her heart still palpitating, and her mind racing, she resigned herself to another half-sleepless night, all courtesy of the teenager she'd agreed to let live with her.

I think I got better sleep when I was being hunted by a serial killer.

The gallows humor made her chuckle to herself but didn't make her any sleepier.

"I didn't do it," Hannah insisted angrily.

Jessie sat across the breakfast table from her, stunned. She couldn't believe the girl was denying it.

"Hannah, there are only two people living here. I went to bed before you did. When I said goodnight, you were watching TV. When I was woken up in the middle of the night, it was on. You don't have to work for the LAPD to know who's responsible for that."

Hannah stared at her, her green eyes full of conviction.

"Jessie, I don't want to be disrespectful. But you admitted that you've had trouble sleeping lately. And at your age, memory starts to falter a little. Is it possible that you're forgetting something *you* actually did, and are blaming it on me because you're buying into the stereotype of the lazy, forgetful teenager?"

Jessie stared back, dumbfounded at Hannah's boldness. It was a stunning move, to lie about something so obvious, for no discernible reason.

"You know I track serial killers for a living, right?" she reminded her. "I'm not exactly susceptible to gaslighting from you."

Hannah took the last bite of her toast and stood up, her sandy-blonde hair falling in her face as she stretched to her full, gangly height of five foot nine, only an inch shorter than Jessie.

"Don't we have to get to that therapist appointment this morning?" she asked, ignoring Jessie's comment completely. "I thought it was at nine. It's eight thirty-two right now."

She headed back to her bedroom to finish getting dressed, leaving her plate and empty cup on the table. Jessie fought the urge to call after her and tell her to toss the stuff in the dishwasher.

She reminded herself of the personal limitations she'd established when Hannah first came to live with her two months ago. She was not, and would not try to be, the girl's parent. Her job was to provide a safe environment for the half-sister she'd never known to recover after a series of traumatizing incidents. Her job was to help Hannah heal and reintegrate into a world that seemed fraught with dangers all around her. Her job was to be a source of support and security. Jessie knew all that instinctively and intellectually, and yet she couldn't help but wonder why the hell the kid couldn't put a frickin' dish away.

As she cleaned up, she told herself for the thousandth time that this was all normal, that Hannah was acting out as a way of asserting control over her own life, something she'd sorely lacked lately, that it wasn't personal and it wouldn't last forever.

She told herself all of these things. But deep down, she wasn't sure she believed any of them. Some part of her worried that there was something darker going on inside Hannah. And she feared that it might be irreversible.

CHAPTER TWO

Jessie was getting antsy.

She knew Hannah's session with Dr. Lemmon would end any second. Would the girl come out of the office crying, like she had on the last visit? Or stone-faced, like after the previous two?

If anyone could reach Hannah, Jessie had to believe it was Dr. Janice Lemmon. Despite her unassuming look, the woman was not to be trifled with. Her small frame, tight blonde perm, and thick glasses made the sixty-something behavioral therapist look more like someone's grandma than one of the most well-regarded experts on aberrant behavior on the West Coast. But underneath that ordinary facade was a woman so highly respected that she still occasionally consulted for the LAPD, the FBI, and other organizations that she never spoke of. She also happened to be Jessie's therapist.

At first, Jessie was concerned that having her treat Hannah as well might be a conflict of interest. But after some discussion, they agreed that there were only a few doctors who were qualified to treat a girl who'd been through Hannah's experiences. And since Dr. Lemmon was already intimately familiar with some of Hannah's family history, she was a logical choice.

After all, it was Dr. Lemmon who had helped Jessie deal with the reality that her father was the notorious serial killer Xander Thurman. It was Dr. Lemmon who talked her through the nightmares and anxiety she suffered as a result of watching her father kill her mother when she was six years old. It was Dr. Lemmon who got her to open up about being left alone by him to die in a snowy cabin, trapped for three days next to the rotting corpse of the woman she had called mommy. It was Dr. Lemmon who helped give her the confidence that she could stand up to her father when he reentered her life twenty-three years later, bent on either converting her into a murderer who would join him or killing her if she wouldn't.

She was the only credible choice of therapists to work with her half-sister, who shared the very same father and equally brutal nightmares. Only a few months ago, Thurman had kidnapped Hannah and her adoptive parents and made the girl watch as he slaughtered them. He'd almost killed Jessie in front of her too. Only their collective quick thinking and grit had turned the tables and left him dead.

But even after that, Hannah's trauma didn't end. Only months after the death of her adoptive parents, an entirely different serial killer named Bolton Crutchfield, an acolyte of her father with a fixation on Jessie, had killed her foster parents in front of her and abducted her. He held her in an isolated basement for a week, trying to indoctrinate her, to mold her into a killer like Thurman and himself.

She survived that horror as well, rescued by Jessie and a clever double-cross of her own. Bolton Crutchfield had been gunned down. And though he was no longer a physical threat, Jessie wasn't as confident that he hadn't wormed his way into Hannah's head, corrupting her with his sick faith, defined by nihilism and blood.

Jessie stood up, in part to stretch but also because she could feel herself sinking into mental quicksand. She looked at herself in the waiting room mirror. She had to admit that, despite spending the last two months as the unexpected guardian of a troubled teenager, she was still presentable.

Her green eyes were bright and clear. Her shoulder-length brown hair was clean, conditioned, and loose, unburdened by her standard work ponytail. A long stretch of not fearing she was being hunted by a serial killer had allowed her to resume a semi-normal workout routine, giving her five-foot-ten-inch frame a strength and solidity it had lost for a while.

Most impressive of all, none of her recent cases had involved shootouts, knife attacks, or anything approaching personal injury. As a result, she hadn't added any new scars to her massive collection, which included a puncture wound in the abdomen, angry lines along both arms and legs, and a long, pinkish moon-shaped scar that ran five inches horizontally along her collarbone from the base of her neck to her right shoulder.

She touched that one unconsciously, wondering if the time might soon be approaching when someone would see it, along with all the others. She could sense that she and Ryan were getting close to the point where they would be able to study each other's physical imperfections up close.

Detective Ryan Hernandez was, in addition to being a colleague she worked cases with regularly, her boyfriend. It felt weird to use the term but there was no way around it. They'd been going out semi-regularly for almost as long as Hannah had been living with her. And though they hadn't taken that final physical step, both of them knew it was close. The anticipation and awkwardness made for an interesting work environment.

Jessie was jolted out of her thoughts by the opening door. Out stepped Hannah, looking neither upset nor closed off. She looked oddly...normal, which, considering everything she'd been through, seemed odd in and of itself.

Dr. Lemmon followed her out and caught Jessie's eye.

"Hannah," she said. "I want to talk to Jessie for a few minutes. Do you mind waiting here briefly?"

"Not at all," Hannah replied, sitting down. "You two come on out when you're done deciding just how crazy I am. I'll just be alerting the state to your massive HIPAA violations."

"Sounds good," Dr. Lemmon said warmly, not taking the bait. "Come on in, Jessie."

Jessie settled into the same loveseat she used for her own sessions and Dr. Lemmon sat down in the chair across from her.

"I want to keep this brief," Dr. Lemmon said. "Despite her sarcasm, I don't think it helps for Hannah to worry that I'm sharing details of what she says with you, even though I assured her I wouldn't."

"Wouldn't or couldn't?" Jessie pressed.

"She's still under eighteen so technically, as her guardian, you could insist. But I think that would undermine the trust I'm trying to develop with her. It's taken a while to get her to open up in any real way. I don't want to put that at risk."

"Understood," Jessie said. "So why am I in here at all?"

"Because I'm worried. Without getting into specifics, I'll just say that apart from one session where she displayed a bit of emotion at what she's been through, Hannah's been largely...unruffled. In retrospect, after having gotten to know her, I suspect that single display of emotion may have been for my benefit. Hannah seems to have disassociated herself from the events that transpired, as if she was an observer of them, rather than a participant."

"That doesn't seem surprising," Jessie said. "In fact, it feels uncomfortably familiar to me."

"As well it should," Dr. Lemmon agreed. "You went through a period like that yourself. It's a fairly common way for the brain to make sense of personal trauma. Compartmentalizing or disconnecting from traumatic events isn't unusual. What worries me is that Hannah doesn't seem to be doing that as a way to protect herself from the pain of what happened to her. She seems to have simply erased the pain from her system, almost like a hard drive that's been wiped. It's as if she doesn't view what she suffered through as suffering so much as simply things that happened. She's narcotized herself from viewing them as things that have anything to do with herself or her family."

"And I'm guessing that's not super healthy?" Jessie mulled as she shifted nervously in her seat.

"I'm loath to put a judgment on it," Dr. Lemmon said in her usual measured style. "It seems to be working for her. My concern is where it can lead. People who aren't able to tap into their own emotional pain occasionally escalate to a point where they can't recognize anyone else's pain, emotional or physical. Their ability to feel empathy disintegrates. That can often lead to socially unacceptable behavior."

"What you're describing sounds like sociopathy," Jessie pointed out.

"Yes," Dr. Lemmon agreed. "Sociopaths do exhibit some of those hallmarks. I wouldn't formally diagnose Hannah as such based on our limited time together. Much of this could simply be attributed to deep-seated PTSD. All the same, have you noticed any behavior that might dovetail with what I've described?"

Jessie thought about the last few months, starting with the inexplicable, pointless lie about the television this morning. She recalled how Hannah had complained when Jessie insisted on taking a sick stray kitten they'd found hiding under an alley dumpster to a vet. She remembered how the girl would go silent for hours, no matter what Jessie did to draw her out. She thought about the time she took Hannah to the gym and how her half-sister had started punching the heavy bag without any gloves, pummeling the thing until her hands were raw and bleeding.

All those behaviors seemed to match Dr. Lemmon's description. But they could all just as easily be interpreted as a young woman working out her inner pain. None of it meant she was a budding sociopath. She didn't want to get anywhere near that label, not even with Dr. Lemmon.

"No," she lied.

The therapist looked at her, obviously unconvinced. But she didn't press, moving on to another priority.

"What about school?" she asked.

"She started up last week. I placed her in that therapeutic high school you recommended."

"Yes, she and I discussed it briefly," Dr. Lemmon acknowledged. "She didn't sound overly impressed. Is that your sense as well?"

"I believe the way she put it was 'how long do I have to hang out with these drug addicts and suicides-in-waiting before I can go back to a real school?'"

Lemmon nodded, clearly not surprised.

"I see," she said. "She was slightly less forthright with me. I understand her frustration. But I think we need to keep her in a secure, highly supervised environment for at least a month before we consider transitioning her back into a traditional high school."

"I get that. But I know she's frustrated. She was supposed to graduate this year. But with all the time she's missed, even at a traditional high school, she's going to have to go to summer school. She isn't psyched to finish up with, as she called them, 'the burnouts and halfwits.'"

"One step at a time," Dr. Lemmon said, unflustered. "Let's move on. How are you doing?"

Jessie laughed despite herself. Where to begin? Before she could, Dr. Lemmon continued.

"We obviously don't have time for a full session right now. But how are you managing? You're suddenly responsible for a minor, you're navigating a new relationship with a co-worker, your job requires you to get in the heads of brutal murderers, and you're dealing with the emotional fallout of ending the lives of two serial killers, one of whom was your father. That's a lot to juggle."

Jessie forced a smile.

"When you put it like that, it does sound like a lot."

Dr. Lemmon didn't smile back.

"I'm serious, Jessie. You need to stay aware of your own mental health. This isn't just a dangerous time for Hannah. The risk of you backsliding is significant as well. Don't be cavalier about that."

Jessie dropped the smile but kept the stiff upper lip.

"I'm aware of the risks, Doc. And I'm doing the best I can to take care of myself. But it's not like I can take a spa day. The world keeps coming at me. And if I stop moving, I'm going to get run over."

"I'm not sure that's true, Jessie," Dr. Lemmon said softly. "Sometimes if you stop moving, the world circles back around and you can hop back on. You are a person of value but don't be arrogant. You're not so indispensable in this world that you can't hit pause every now and then."

Jessie nodded aggressively, sarcastically.

"Noted," she said, pretending to take notes. "Don't be arrogant. Not indispensable."

Dr. Lemmon pursed her lips, coming as close to annoyed as she was likely to ever reveal. Jessie tried to push past it.

"How's Garland doing?" she asked teasingly.

"I'm sorry?" Dr. Lemmon said.

"You know, Garland Moses, profiling consultant for the LAPD, helped me find and rescue Hannah, older, scruffy-looking in a charming, devil-may-care sort of way."

"I'm familiar with Mr. Moses, Jessie. I'm just not sure why you're asking me about him."

"No reason," Jessie said, sensing she'd hit a nerve. "He just mentioned you a while back and something about his tone gave me the impression that you two were chummy. So I was wondering how he was doing?"

"I think that will complete our time today," Dr. Lemmon said brusquely.

"Wow," Jessie said, smiling for real now. "You really shut that down fast, Doc."

Dr. Lemmon stood up and motioned for them to head to the exit. Jessie decided to ease up. As they reached the door, she turned back to the therapist and asked the question that had been eating at her for the last few minutes.

"Seriously, Doc, if Hannah is heading down a road where she has trouble feeling empathy for other people, is there any way to reverse that?"

Dr. Lemmon paused and looked her squarely in the eye.

"Jessie, I've spent thirty-five years of my life trying to answer questions like that. The best answer I can give you is: I hope so."

CHAPTER THREE

Lizzie Polacnyk got home seriously late.

She'd expected to be back from her study group session at California State University—Northridge by 7 p.m. But they had a big Psychology 101 exam tomorrow and everyone was quizzing each other relentlessly. When they called it quits for the night, it was after nine.

By the time she opened the apartment front door, it was almost 9:45. She tried to keep quiet, remembering that Michaela had a 6 a.m. call time both earlier this morning and tomorrow and was probably fast asleep by now.

She tiptoed down the hallway to her bedroom and was surprised to see a dim light leaking out from under Michaela's door. It wasn't like her to stay up late when she had to be up by 5 a.m. She wondered if her longtime friend and more recent roommate had simply been so tired that she fell asleep with the light on. She decided to peek in and turn it off if need be.

When she cracked open the door slightly, she saw Michaela lying on her back without the covers on. Her pillow partially obscured her face. She only had the reading lamp on so it was hard to be sure but it looked like she hadn't even changed out of her outfit from the day, a cheerleading uniform.

Lizzie was about to close the door when she noticed something odd. The skirt was riding down near Michaela's thighs so that her crotch was exposed. That seemed inappropriate, no matter how exhausted she was.

Lizzie debated whether to throw a sheet over her friend. Considering what Michaela did for a living, it seemed like forced modesty. Besides, it wasn't like anyone else was going to walk in on her. Still, Lizzie felt her Catholic girls school upbringing kicking in and knew it would gnaw at her all night if she did nothing.

So she gently pushed the door open and stepped inside, quietly walking over to the side of the bed. She got halfway there when she stopped cold. Now with an unobstructed view, she saw the gaping holes in Michaela's chest and stomach.

A thick, wet pool of blood had oozed out of the sliced up uniform and surrounded her entire torso, slowly seeping into the bed sheets. Michaela's eyes were clenched tight, as if keeping them closed could have protected her from whatever happened.

Lizzie stood there for several seconds, unsure how to react. She felt like she should scream but her throat had suddenly gone dry. Her stomach gurgled and she briefly feared she might throw up.

Feeling like she was in a strange dream, she turned and walked out of the bedroom and back into the kitchen, where she poured herself a glass of water. When she was confident that she would be able to speak, she called 911.

The date was going well.

In the back of her mind, Jessie started to wonder if tonight might be the night. She was almost reluctant to wish for it. Her relationship with Ryan was the most stable thing in her life right now and she was hesitant to do anything to complicate it.

She'd spent most of the evening at the charmingly cheesy Italian restaurant complaining about how things were going with Hannah. She recounted the basics of her conversation with Dr. Lemmon and lamented the lack of forward progress they were making in helping her half-sister adjust to her new normal. It was only when Ryan excused himself to go to the restroom and she looked around the restaurant that Jessie realized just how self-centered she'd been.

The place, a legendary if cheesy San Fernando Valley haunt called Miceli's, was darkly lit and romantic. The vibe was heightened by the fact that Ryan had somehow secured the one table on the second floor, in what amounted to an indoor balcony overlooking the rest of the restaurant. But until now, she'd been mostly oblivious.

She'd also barely registered until he left that he'd hardly spoken all night. Instead he sat patiently as she prattled on about her domestic troubles, barely letting him get in a word. In fact, now that she thought about it, she didn't recall asking him a single question all evening.

As the guilt washed over her, she saw him leave the restroom on the floor below and deftly navigate his way through the maze of tables to the stairs. As he did, she noticed something else—almost every woman who could get away with it cast a glance his way. Who could blame them?

The man was hard to ignore. Six feet tall and two hundred pounds of what looked like marble, with unassuming, short black hair and welcoming brown eyes, he walked with the quiet confidence of a man who didn't need to impress anyone.

And if these women knew what he did for a living, they'd be even more intrigued. As the lead detective for a special unit of the LAPD called Homicide Special Section—HSS for short—his cases all had high profiles or intense media scrutiny, often involving multiple victims and serial killers.

And he was here with her. It had taken a while to get to this point. He was in the final stages of a divorce after six years of marriage. Jessie had been single a little longer. Her marriage had ended more dramatically, when her now ex-husband attempted to frame her for killing his mistress. When she'd uncovered his plan, he tried to kill her. He was currently incarcerated in a prison in Orange County.

Ryan sat down across from her and she reached for his hand.

"I'm sorry," she said. "I've been totally dominating the conversation. How are you?"

"I'm okay," he said. "That drug kingpin assassination wrapped up today."

"You never called me in to help," she noted, pretending to be hurt.

"It was pretty cut and dried. We didn't really need the services of any fancy profiler for that one."

"Who cares?" Jessie protested. "Call me in anyway. At least then we can spend a little time together, even if I might have to bail at some point."

"How romantic," he said. "Nothing like making googly eyes over a dead body."

"We do what we've got to do," she said, shrugging. "Besides, for my last case I was assigned to work with Trembley, who—no offense—isn't exactly my dream partner."

"Hey," Ryan mock-protested. "Detective Alan Trembley is a solid professional and you should be honored to work with him on any case you're assigned."

"He's quite boring."

"I resent that on his behalf," he said, trying to scowl. "Besides, not having you with me allows me to plan your birthday without you hovering."

"You're planning something for me?" Jessie asked, genuinely surprised. "I didn't even know you knew when it was."

"I'm a detective, Jessie. That's kind of in my wheelhouse. I wouldn't even mention it except that I need you to make sure your schedule is clear on Thursday evening. Cool?"

"Cool," she agreed, blushing slightly.

He smiled back and she felt a rush of warmth come over her. Someone going to the trouble to learn her birthday and organize something for it would normally have made Jessie illogically anxious. But somehow, because it was Ryan, she felt comfortable with the idea, even excited.

She wondered if he might be planning an early gift of an intimate nature for her tonight. She was about to hint at the idea when his phone rang. She didn't recognize the ringtone. Whoever it was caused Ryan to frown. He mouthed *sorry* as he picked up.

"Detective Hernandez," he said.

Jessie watched as Ryan listened to the voice on the other end of the line. The frown on his face became more pronounced with each passing moment. After waiting silently for about thirty seconds, he finally responded.

"But Valley Division's already there. Won't it be too late?"

He was quiet as the other person responded. After another twenty seconds, he spoke again.

"I understand. I'm on it."

Then he hung up. He stared at the phone for a moment as if it might speak directly to him. When he looked up, his eyes were steely.

"I hate to do this but we have to skip dessert. I have to check out a crime scene and if we don't leave now, it might be too late."

Jessie had rarely seen Ryan look so uneasy. He waved at the server to get her attention, handing her a pile of bills from his wallet when she hurried over.

"Too late?" Jessie asked. "What does that mean?"

Ryan stood up and indicated that she should do the same. He was already headed for the stairs when he replied.

"I'll explain on the way."

CHAPTER FOUR

Jessie forced herself to wait.

Whatever this was about, it had Ryan on edge and she didn't want to make it worse. She sat quietly in the passenger seat, allowing him to reveal what was going on when he felt comfortable.

"Are you sure you're okay coming?" he asked again.

"Yes," she assured him. "I texted Hannah that a case came up and that she shouldn't expect me back before she goes to bed. We're good."

"You could have rideshared from the restaurant," he reminded her.

"I wanted to come, Ryan," she insisted, again biting her tongue despite the desire to ask additional questions.

He continued west on Ventura Boulevard deeper into the Valley. After another ten seconds of silence, he finally began to speak.

"So here's the deal. I have a contact in the department who will occasionally alert me to cases I should be aware of."

"Could you be a little *more* cryptic?" Jessie asked, unable to contain herself.

"I actually don't have much more than that to share," he said, ignoring her snark. "About four years ago, I got a call from a burner phone. The voice was digitally manipulated. The caller suggested that the prime suspect in the murder of a wealthy businessman was being set up and that I should look at political motivations for the killing."

"This call just came out of the blue?" she asked.

"Yep. I was a junior grade detective without much to lose so I followed it up. The case was about to be closed. But I started asking questions and pretty quickly, the whole thing unraveled. It turned out that the businessman was a major supporter and fundraiser for a local city councilman. Once he died, the councilman's funding dried up. His challenger was able to overwhelm him financially and won the seat. In the end, we realized the challenger for the seat had hired someone to take out the businessman for exactly that reason, to kneecap the incumbent's primary source of financial support. He also had the original suspect framed so it would look like a random robbery gone wrong."

"How did your contact know all that?"

"I have no idea. I'm not even sure the source knew the extent of the thing. I got the sense that the person, who I started calling Chatty Cathy, knew something was off, even if the details were hazy."

"Is the source a woman?"

"No way to tell," Ryan admitted. "But for the purpose of giving them a name, let's say yes. Anyway, I started to get additional calls after that. Not often, maybe twice a year. They were always from burners using digital voice masking. And they almost always involved cases that seemed open and shut, but upon further investigation, were more complicated."

"So Chatty Cathy is some sort of guardian against injustice?"

"Maybe," Ryan said, not sounding as confident. "Or it could be something else. I've noticed that in most of these cases, the real story is messy and makes people in positions of power look bad. A lot of times, I think our higher-ups would rather go for the easy answer than get into the muck of uncovering crimes that might implicate folks with influence. By calling me, Chatty Cathy gets to raise the alarm about questionable cases without getting herself dirty or putting her career at risk. The goal may be noble but I think there's some self-interest involved too."

"So what about this case made her reach out?"

"I don't know," Ryan said as he turned right off Ventura Boulevard onto Coldwater Canyon Avenue. "She never tells me why a case is sketchy, just that it is. All I know is that a woman was murdered in the thirteen thousand block of Bessemer Street in Van Nuys. She was stabbed multiple times in the torso. The preliminary theory is that it was a robbery gone wrong; that the burglar didn't think anyone was home and attacked the resident upon finding her."

"Do they have a suspect?"

"They don't," Ryan said. "But according to Chatty Cathy, things are moving fast. The nine-one-one call only came in about a half hour ago and the coroner is already on scene, preparing to remove the body."

"The detectives are okay with that?" Jessie asked, incredulous.

"My understanding is that they aren't even there yet. The senior uniformed officer gave the order."

"What?" Jessie said, dumbfounded. "That'll compromise the crime scene. Can we stop that?"

"That's why I said we had to leave right away," Ryan replied. "Chatty Cathy said the coroner was trying to slow down the process but that we have about ten minutes before they have no choice but to bag the body."

"How far away are we?" Jessie asked.

"Not far," Ryan said as he turned onto a residential street doused in flashing lights. "It's that building halfway up the block."

They parked a few doors down and got out. Hurrying over, Jessie couldn't help but notice that despite the lights, there weren't as many vehicles as she would have expected. There was the coroner's van, an ambulance, and two squad cars. Usually a murder scene would have at least double that many black-and-whites.

As they approached the building, the lone uniformed officer outside gave them a wary look. Ryan flashed his badge.

"What's the story, Officer?" he asked.

Considering the time constraints, Jessie was surprised that Ryan was stopping at all. The young African-American officer, who couldn't have been more than twenty-five, had a nervous expression and the name tag Burnside.

"Sir," he answered, his voice cracking slightly, "we've got a Caucasian female, seventeen, multiple stab wounds to her chest and abdomen. She was found in her bed by her roommate."

"Are the Valley Bureau detectives on scene yet?" Ryan asked.

"No sir."

"Who's in charge then?"

"That would be my boss, Sergeant Costabile from Van Nuys Station," the officer answered as he pointed back to the right. "He's inside. It's apartment 116."

"Thanks," Ryan said briskly, grimacing slightly as he walked by with Jessie right behind.

"Do you know Costabile?" Jessie asked as she hurried to match his pace.

"Only by reputation," Ryan said. "Hank Costabile's not just old school, he's ancient. And from what I hear, he's a pit bull."

"Pit bulls are actually agreeable by nature," Jessie said a little indignantly.

"Point taken," Ryan said. "But you know what I'm saying. He's known to be ... difficult. This could get ugly so be prepared."

"What does that mean?" Jessie demanded.

But before he could answer they had reached the door. A burly officer named Lester stood just outside the taped off unit. He looked as wary as the cop outside but less nervous. Jessie observed that Ryan didn't show his badge to this guy.

"This area is off limits," Officer Lester said brusquely. "Police business. The officer outside should have told you."

"Oh yeah?" Ryan whispered in a curious, very un-detectivelike tone. "What happened? You can tell me."

"I'm not at liberty to say," Lester snapped. "Are you a resident of this building, sir? Because we can't have civilians just wandering through a crime scene."

"Oh no, we wouldn't want that," Ryan agreed smarmily. "That'd be almost as bad as removing a dead body before the assigned detectives got a chance to evaluate the scene. Am I right?"

The officer narrowed his eyes at the question, now fully aware that something unusual was going on.

"Who are you, sir?" he asked, his brusqueness now laced with a hint of apprehension.

"I'm sure as hell not a Valley Bureau detective," Ryan said, his voice booming.

"Sir ..." the officer began, clearly flummoxed.

"It's okay, Lester," said a bald, barrel-chested officer who walked up behind him. "Don't you know who that is? It's the famed detective Ryan Hernandez from Central Station. You can let him in. But be sure to get his autograph before he leaves."

"Sergeant Costabile, I assume?" Ryan asked, his eyebrows raised.

"That's right," Costabile said with a sneering grin. "To what do we owe the honor of your presence, Detective? Showing your long-legged, pretty lady friend how the other half lives out here in the Valley?"

"My 'long-legged, pretty lady friend' is actually criminal profiler Jessie Hunt. You know, she's the one who catches serial killers almost as often as you catch venereal diseases."

There was a long, uncomfortable silence in which Jessie thought Costabile might simply pull out his gun and shoot Ryan. The man's nasty grin faded so that it was now a nasty scowl. After what felt like an eternity, the sergeant gave a loud, forced guffaw.

"I guess I deserved that," he said, glancing over at Jessie, not sounding even mildly chastened. "It was rude of me to be so dismissive of you, Ms. Hunt. Your reputation precedes you. I can only imagine what law enforcement lottery allowed us to be graced with your singular genius this evening. Pray tell, what brings you here?"

Jessie wanted desperately to respond to the mockery with some of her own but didn't want to upset whatever plan Ryan clearly had in mind. So she choked down her disdain.

"I'm afraid I can't be completely forthcoming," she said apologetically. "But I'll let Detective Hernandez share what he's able to."

"Thanks, Ms. Hunt," Ryan said, smoothly taking the baton. "We just happened to be in the area wrapping up an interview when we got the alert about this case. It sounded like it might be part of a pattern we're investigating and we thought we'd check it out firsthand."

"You think this is related to a case you're working?" Costabile asked disbelievingly.

"It's possible," Ryan said. "We'd have to look at the body to draw any firm conclusions. Of course, we don't want to step on the toes of the detectives already assigned. Who might that be?"

Costabile stared at Ryan, taking note of his challenging tone. It was clear that Ryan knew there were no detectives on the scene yet. Costabile appeared to be debating whether to answer the spoken question seriously or address the one below the surface about what exactly was going on here.

"Detective Strode should be here momentarily," he finally said in a disturbingly polite tone. "But we were prepping the body to be viewed down at the coroner's. Everything looks pretty open and shut. We didn't want to waste department resources unnecessarily."

"Sure, sure. I get it," Ryan replied, using the same official but not genuine politeness as Costabile. "All the same, maybe we take a look here so as to not compromise the scene. We *are* talking about a teenage girl stabbed in her own bed ... how many times?"

Costabile's face turned red and it looked like it was taking an enormous effort for him to keep his composure.

"Nine . . . that we're aware of."

"Nine times?" Ryan repeated. "That seems like a lot. Doesn't that seem like a lot to you, Ms. Hunt?"

"It seems like a lot," Jessie agreed.

"Yeah, a lot," Ryan added for emphasis. "So maybe we dot the 'i's' and cross the 't's' on this one before tossing the girl into a plastic bag and driving her over a bunch of pothole-strewn Valley streets? You know, just to be thorough."

He smiled sweetly as if he'd merely been discussing the weather. Costabile did not smile back.

"Are you taking over this investigation, Detective?" the sergeant asked flatly, not commenting on the pothole dig.

"Not at this point, Sergeant. Like I said, we just want to see if the killing fits our pattern. You're not denying us access to the body, are you?"

That question led to another uncomfortable silence. Jessie watched another officer named Webb wander over from inside the apartment and take up a position right behind Costabile. His right hand was resting uncomfortably close to his gun holster. She glanced back and saw that Officer Lester had now stepped inside the police tape and was standing behind them, assuming the same posture with his hand in the same position.

Costabile looked down at his shoes and kept his gaze there for several seconds. Ryan stared at the top of the man's head, his eyes unblinking. Jessie was afraid to breathe. Finally, Costabile looked up. A vein on his forehead bulged. His eyes were angry slits. Slowly, he opened them and his body seemed to relax slightly.

"Come on in," he said, waving his hand in an exaggerated welcome.

Ryan stepped forward and Jessie followed. As she moved into the apartment, she reminded herself it was okay to breathe again.

CHAPTER FIVE

I t was hard to stay focused.

With so much testosterone bouncing around the apartment, Jessie was still slightly apprehensive that a shootout might break out any moment.

She tried to force the simmering animosity out of her brain as she walked through the place. She needed to have a clear head from this point forward. The coroner might focus on the state of the body and the crime scene folks might look for blood spatter or fingerprints. But she needed to be aware of everything that contributed to the psychological makeup of the victim. Even the smallest detail could lead to the killer.

The apartment was fairly unremarkable. It was clear to her from the décor that both residents were female even though the gender of the victim's roommate hadn't been mentioned. One of them was clearly way more personally conservative than the other. The wall art was a confusing amalgam of watercolors and religious iconography next to Gustav Klimt prints and incendiary Mapplethorpe photos.

As she walked down the hall, Jessie got the distinct sense that the more outré roommate was also the one with more money. Her style seemed far more dominant. When they passed the smaller bedroom, she glanced in and saw a cross on the wall above the dresser.

So the one who could afford the bigger bedroom died.

Sure enough, they continued on to the larger bedroom at the end of the hall, from where she could hear voices.

"You up for this, criminal profiler lady?" Costabile asked derisively.

"She's been . . ." Ryan started to say but she cut him off.

"I'm good," she answered.

She didn't need him standing up for her professional virtue. And she definitely didn't want another tough guy competition when she was trying to concentrate. Ignoring whatever stare-down was going on behind her, she took a deep breath and stepped into the bedroom.

Before even looking at the body, she allowed her eyes to scan the room. There were more of the bold decorating choices on the walls and a disco ball lamp beside the bed. A chair in the corner was on its side and magazines were scattered on the floor, hinting at a struggle. The desk was mostly empty, though there was a clean, rectangular spot surrounded by a layer of dust, a sure sign that a laptop had recently been there.

"TV is still here," Ryan noted. "So is the gaming console. Seems like an odd decision for a thief to leave that stuff."

"Laptop is gone though," Jessie noted. "Anyone find a cell phone?"

"Not yet," Officer Webb said.

"Did you get her number from the roommate so we can try to track it?" she asked, trying not to let her impatience show.

"The roommate has been a little on the hysterical side," Costabile said. "We've had trouble getting much of anything out of her other than her name, Elizabeth Polacnyk. The EMTs have her in the ambulance outside. They were going to sedate her."

"Okay," Jessie said. "But don't let her leave until we've had a chance to speak to her."

Costabile still looked put out but nodded for Officer Lester, who was still near the front door, to convey the demand. As he did, Jessie finally turned her attention to the girl on the bed. She was already in the body bag, though it hadn't been zipped up. The sight of it was infuriating to Jessie.

"Did anyone take photos before her body was disturbed?" Ryan asked, speaking aloud the question in Jessie's head.

A crime scene tech raised his hand.

"I managed to snap a few just before she was loaded in the bag," he said.

The deputy medical examiner on the case walked over.

"Hi. I'm Maggie Caldwell. We tried to hold off on bagging," she said apologetically. "But we were instructed otherwise."

The accusation hung in the air, unspoken.

"Like I said," Costabile said defensively, "seemed like an open-and-shut case; didn't want to waste resources."

Jessie tried to keep her voice even as she replied.

"I'm sure you have decades of experience on the job, Sergeant," she said. "But are you in the habit of making the command decision to disturb a murder scene before the detectives arrive, regardless of what resources it requires?"

"Valley Bureau isn't as flush as you Downtown types," he barked. "We don't have the luxury of lingering lovingly over every dead runaway we find."

As Jessie's temper flared, she found her voice getting calmer and slower.

"I wasn't aware that police procedure in this part of town now placed budget savings over crime-solving. I'd love to see where that line is in the new regulations. Additionally, I didn't realize that the murders of teen runaways weren't worth investigating. Did I miss that day at LAPD regulations school?"

"Are you questioning my professionalism?" Costabile asked, taking a step toward her.

"I'm just asking questions, Sergeant," she answered, not backing up. "If your conscience is suggesting something deeper, that's for you to work out. I would note that if this girl is a teen runaway, she's doing pretty well. It's clear that she's got a well-paying job that allows her to live in a sizable apartment, buy art, and, based on her nails and hair, get expensive salon care. Are you sure you're not making assumptions about her background?"

Costabile looked like he didn't know which challenging question to address first. After a moment of frustrated huffing, he responded.

"The girl was found in a cheerleader uniform with the skirt down. Feels pretty trashy to me. My guess is she's a working girl."

"No chance that the skirt was pulled down by her assailant?" Jessie mused. "Your officer said she was seventeen. No chance she's a high school cheerleader? No chance she's an actress in costume? We're sure she's a trash whore? You seem to be making a lot of assumptions for an experienced law enforcement professional, Sergeant."

Costabile took another step forward. He was now face to face with her. Jessie worried that Ryan might try to intervene but he held back. She suspected he knew what she was doing. Costabile spoke at her under his breath.

"So you're gonna come in here with your hipster, hot-to-trot profiling rep and call me out as bad at my job? That's where we're at now?"

He was almost growling but Jessie didn't care.

"If the shoe fits," she whispered. "Also, if you think you can intimidate me with your man boobs and garlic breath, you're mistaken. I've gone toe to toe with guys who kept human body parts as souvenirs, so your cheap bullying tactics don't impress me. Now get the hell out of my face."

Costabile's nostrils flared. The blood vessel on his forehead looked like it might pop at any second. Jessie watched him closely. Part of her wanted to knee him in the crotch. But her analytical side was still testing him, trying to determine exactly what was going on here and why procedure wasn't being followed. Something was very off. If he got angry enough, maybe the guy would inadvertently reveal something.

The two of them glared at each other. Costabile was hunkered and wheezy; Jessie silent and taut. She was happy to stay like that all evening if it broke him. After a good five seconds, he exhaled, intentionally breathing on her. He plastered a forced smile onto his face and took a step back.

"I have to say, Ms. Hunt, you are an even bigger bitch than I'd heard you were."

"What's her name?" Jessie demanded almost before he could finish his insult.

"What?" he said, startled by her sudden response.

"The girl," she pressed, nodding at the bed. "Do you even know her name?"

"Her name is Michaela Penn," Officer Lester said, rescuing his superior from potential embarrassment. "We're still digging up info but it looks like she went to a local Catholic girls high school. She became an emancipated minor almost two years ago and graduated early. She was waitressing part-time at Jerry's Deli in Studio City."

"Thanks, Officer," Jessie said, before adding one more line for Sergeant Costabile's benefit. "Sounds real trashy."

She turned and really looked at Michaela closely for the first time since entering the room. The first thing that jumped out at her was just how young the girl looked. She may have been seventeen, but with her short, dark hair and pale, now-bluish skin, she looked closer to fifteen.

She glanced up at a photo of the girl on the dresser and tried to reconcile it with the lifeless form on the bed. The Michaela in the picture was beautiful in a delicately pixie-ish way. She reminded Jessie of a girl from those Japanese anime cartoons.

Her deep blue eyes were huge but unemotional, as if she'd learned to hide her emotions long ago. Only the slight half-smirk at the edges of her lips hinted at what might be hidden beneath. She gave off the vibe of an unlit firework, like she was just biding her time, ready to explode at any moment.

"Can you unzip the bag?" Ryan asked as she moved over next to Jessie. As they waited he muttered under his breath. "I hope permanently alienating the most connected uniformed officer in the Valley was worth whatever you were trying to uncover by insulting him. Because he's never going to let this go."

"Jury's still out," she murmured back.

The cops had moved away but Maggie Caldwell, the deputy medical examiner, remained close by after she unzipped the bag.

"Sorry," she said quietly. "I didn't want to touch the body but Costabile was adamant that we move quickly. If you'd arrived five minutes later, she'd have been packed up in the van."

"Any idea what the rush was?" Ryan asked her.

"No," Caldwell said nervously. "But I don't think it was all his idea. He was on the phone with someone who seemed to be giving him instructions. It was after he hung up that he really tried to push things along."

Jessie moved closer to the girl. Her cheerleading uniform, red, with white script and black trim, was nondescript. The writing said only "Central H.S." The skirt was pulled down to her thighs.

"Lester said she already graduated, right?" Ryan recalled. "So why the uniform?"

"I've lived in this area for twenty years and I don't recognize that school or those colors," Caldwell said. "I don't think it's real."

"Maybe it was a costume," Jessie suggested. "Waitressing and acting are hardly mutually exclusive."

"Possible," Ryan agreed. "I hate to say it, but Costabile could be right too. It could be an outfit she wore for... a client. That wouldn't be unheard of around here."

Jessie nodded, voicing her own theory.

"Whatever she was doing, unless she had a trust fund, it was more than just waitressing. This place is nice. The art isn't cheap and it's clear that she had a comprehensive skin and hair regimen that involved professional assistance. She wasn't struggling. Do we know if she was sexually assaulted?" she asked Caldwell.

"Too early to tell. We'll know more tomorrow."

"We should definitely talk to the roommate soon," Ryan said. "Maybe she can let us know if Michaela had received any threats recently."

Jessie nodded in agreement as she looked more closely at the knife puncture wounds. There were five in the chest and another four in the abdomen.

"Did anyone find the murder weapon?" she asked.

"There's a butcher knife missing from the kitchen set," Officer Lester, who had overheard the question, volunteered. "But we haven't been able to locate it."

"That's weird," Ryan noted.

"What?" Lester asked.

"Well, if this was a robbery gone wrong, you'd expect the perpetrator to be surprised to find Michaela in her room. The general disarray in this room suggests a struggle. But if the perp didn't know she was here, how did he get the knife? It's hard to believe he ran back to the kitchen to get it and then came back to the bedroom again."

"Maybe he knocked her out and then got the knife?" Lester offered.

"But if he knocked her out and this was a robbery, why not just take the stuff and go?" Jessie wondered. "There wouldn't be any resistance at that point. To go grab a knife, return to the bedroom, and stab an unconscious girl nine times. That doesn't sound like typical robber behavior. That's cold-blooded. And yet..."

"What?" Lester prodded.

"A laptop was taken," she said, nodding at the empty desk. "And we don't have her phone here. So she *was* robbed. The question is: was that an afterthought? Was it staged or were those things taken for a specific reason? Whatever the case, it's hardly open and shut."

That last comment made Costabile, who'd been standing quietly in the corner for the last few minutes, perk up.

"I thought you were done casting aspersions for a few minutes," he said acidly. "But I guess it was too much to hope for."

Jessie was about to retort when Ryan stepped in.

"We'll let it lie for now," he said. "After all, we still need to talk to the roommate. Come on, Jessie."

They started for the door. But Ryan stopped just as they were leaving. Leaning in so that only she and Costabile could hear him, he muttered one last thing to the man.

"But I have to tell you, Sergeant, if you think we're done asking why you're handling this case in such rushed, slipshod fashion, you are sadly mistaken. I don't know what you're hiding, but this case stinks. If you think you can keep a lid on it, you're kidding yourself."

Costabile didn't reply. But he did give Ryan a big, toothy, malevolent grin that suggested he felt otherwise.

Chapter Six

For a second, Jessie thought Michaela's roommate was dead too.

Despite the EMTs' assurances to the contrary, she was unresponsive when they opened the ambulance door and tried to get her attention. Even after they called her by what the EMT said was her preferred name, Lizzie, she didn't stir. It was only when Ryan pulled off the thermal blanket she was wrapped in that she gave them the time of day.

"What?" she demanded in a tired, surly voice.

The girl looked to be in her late teens. Even if she hadn't seen Lizzie's room, Jessie would have guessed she was a more restrained personality than her roommate. Her brown hair was tied back tight and her makeup was subdued to the point of unnoticeable. She was dressed conservatively in a zippered CSUN sweatshirt and pants. She wore a crucifix necklace.

Jessie frowned at Ryan, not pleased with his tactics. But he shrugged as if to say he was done being patient.

"Lizzie," Jessie began, using her most sympathetic voice, "we're investigating what happened and we need to ask you a few questions."

"They gave me something," Lizzie said. "I'm feeling a little loopy."

"We understand," Jessie assured as she helped the girl up to a seated position. "And we're going to have you go to the hospital to get checked out momentarily. But we need to get some basics from you first, okay?"

"I guess."

"How did you know Michaela?" Jessie asked.

"We went to high school together," Lizzie said, speaking slowly as she focused on each word. "She left early but we stayed in touch. When I graduated we decided to become roomies. She was a good roomie."

Jessie glanced over at Ryan. The girl was really zonked out. Getting much out of her would be hard. He raised his eyebrows in frustration. Jessie tried again.

"Lizzie, did Michaela have family in the area?"

With much effort, Lizzie shook her head.

"What about a boyfriend or someone she recently broke up with?"

"No boyfriend," Lizzie answered lazily.

"Maybe a co-worker she had problems with?"

Lizzie's eyes, which had been glazed over, briefly focused.

"Mick was a waitress," she said adamantly.

"Okay," Jessie replied, surprised by the intensity of the response. "Did she have any issues with anyone at work?"

"She was a waitress," Lizzie repeated vehemently.

Jessie gave up and turned back to Ryan.

"I think we're going to have to wait to talk to her. This is pointless."

"That would be my preference anyway," said the EMT, who had been standing nearby. "After what she's been through, and with the medication she's on, I'd really like to get her looked at."

"Go ahead," Ryan told him. "We'll come by to talk to her tomorrow."

They watched as Lizzie was strapped into a stretcher and the ambulance doors closed. As the vehicle pulled away into the dark night, something occurred to Jessie.

"The Valley detective still hasn't showed up."

"I'm actually not sure we want to be here when he does," Ryan noted. "I don't want him peppering us with questions about the 'investigation pattern' we're pursuing."

"You don't want to ask him why he showed up so late?" Jessie asked, surprised.

"I do. But I have a feeling we'd hit the same brick wall that we got with Costabile. We need to know more before we start coming at these guys."

"I get that," she said. "But just to be clear, we're in agreement that something seriously shady is going on here, right? I mean, that Costabile guy seems more like a mob capo than a police sergeant. Or maybe he's the Don Corleone of Valley Bureau."

Ryan looked over at her, clearly uncomfortable with her words, though he didn't try to argue. She decided to let him off the hook and continued speaking before he could answer.

"I don't think we're likely to get anything useful tonight." She sighed.

"No. We may have to pick this up tomorrow morning. By then, Lizzie will be coherent. Caldwell might have something definitive on a potential sexual assault and we can see if someone tried to pawn Michaela's laptop or phone."

"Okay," Jessie said reluctantly. "One thing we know for sure. Your Chatty Cathy was right. Something definitely isn't right with this case."

Hannah was awake when Jessie got home.

The girl barely looked up from the movie she was watching when she walked in. It was almost I a.m. and tomorrow was a school day but Jessie didn't have the energy to fight.

"It's been a long night," she said. "I'm going to bed. Can you please turn the volume down and try to get some sleep soon so you can function tomorrow?"

Hannah turned the volume down a few notches but otherwise didn't acknowledge her half-sister's words. Jessie stood in her bedroom doorway for a moment, debating whether to try again. But ultimately she decided it wasn't worth it and simply closed the door.

She slept restlessly that night. That wasn't unusual. For the last few years, she could count on near-nightly nightmares centered on one of the men who had posed a threat to her very life. They were usually a mix of her ex-husband, her father, and Bolton Crutchfield.

But tonight, like so many recent nights, her dreams centered on Hannah. Her mind was filled with a swirl of disconnected images, some of the girl in peril at the hands of a masked assailant, others in which she walked nonchalantly into danger.

But the dream that troubled her the most was the last one, in which Hannah sat at a table, smiling casually as an unidentifiable waiter served her a plate filled with dismembered body parts. She was just lifting a forkful of human flesh to her mouth when Jessie startled awake, drenched in sweat and breathing heavily.

The first rays of morning sun streamed in through a crack in the curtains. She sat up, swung her legs over the side of the bed, and rested her head in her hands. Her skull was pounding and she felt vaguely nauseated. As she reached for ibuprofen and a bottle of Pepto-Bismol, she tried not to read too much into the dreams.

She knew from experience that they weren't so much a predictor as a manifestation of her fears. She was having these dreams because she feared for Hannah's future, not because of anything she was destined to become.

At least that's what she told herself.

CHAPTER SEVEN

Despite her exhaustion, Jessie was excited to get to the station.

She managed to get Hannah out the door only ten minutes late this morning and figured that if she hit only light traffic, she could still arrive at work before it got too busy. She wanted some quiet time to focus on the Michaela Penn case, which felt more wrong every time she thought about it.

Why did the officers on scene want to wrap things up so fast? Why hadn't the detective arrived more quickly—if he arrived at all? What made Chatty Cathy call Ryan in the first place? Jessie's gut screamed that this was more than just a standard robbery gone wrong. Nine stab wounds felt very personal.

And yet, as she'd been reminded repeatedly at the ten-week FBI Academy training session she'd attended, her gut was no substitute for evidence. Just because a person or scenario seemed suspicious, that wasn't proof of anything on its own. For Jessie, who had excelled at almost every test they threw at her at Quantico, taking that lesson to heart had been the most challenging.

When she arrived at her desk at 7:33 a.m., the station bullpen was still sparsely populated. She knew she had about a half hour until that changed so she dived right in. First she called the Valley Bureau Coroner's Office to get any results they might have. Maggie Caldwell wasn't in. But according to Jimmy, the guy on call, she'd instructed him to pass along any updates if someone from Central Station called. At least Caldwell didn't seem to be part of whatever slow walk operation Sergeant Costabile was running.

According to Jimmy, Michaela had been sexually assaulted before she died. But apparently the assailant had used a condom and then doused her in some sort of disinfectant that prevented the collection of any usable DNA. They were waiting to see if more detailed testing might offer something but he wasn't optimistic.

Her next call was to the hospital to check on Lizzie. As she waited on hold for an update, her thoughts drifted to back to Hannah. The similarities between her and Michaela Penn weren't lost on her. Both girls were seventeen. Both had gone to private schools in the San Fernando Valley. It looked like both of them had to grow up faster than they should have. Jessie couldn't help but wonder what other parallels they shared.

A nurse came on the line, snapping her out of her thoughts. Apparently Lizzie was still sedated. The nurse said she should be awake by mid-morning and suggested holding off on visiting until then.

After that she called Van Nuys Station and asked for Officer Burnside, who had been standing guard outside the apartment building. Out of all the cops she encountered last night, he was the one who seemed the least comfortable with the situation. She hoped she might be able to pry some details out of him. She was told his shift had just ended—it ran from 7 p.m. to 7 a.m. With a little cajoling, she was able to convince the desk sergeant to give her his cell number. Her hope that he might be awake and still driving home was rewarded when he picked up on the second ring.

"Hello?" he said tentatively.

"Officer Burnside? This is Jessie Hunt. We met last night at the Penn murder scene."

"I know who you are," he said, caution in his voice.

Sensing his intense wariness, she debated whether to try to set him at ease or just accept that this was going to be an uncomfortable situation. She decided that being forthright was the smarter move.

"Look, Officer, I know you're not psyched to be getting this call. And I don't want to put you in a difficult situation, so I'll keep it brief."

She paused, but when she got no response, she continued.

"I'm wondering if you've gotten any updates on the status of Michaela's phone or laptop. Any pings on the phone? Any attempts to pawn it or the computer that you're aware of?"

After a period of silence, Burnside finally responded.

"I think you'd be better off going through official channels, Ms. Hunt."

He sounded embarrassed to say it and she decided to use that to her advantage.

"I think we both know how well that would go, Officer. I'd be running in circles for hours. Look, I'm not asking you to tell me why that crime scene was handled so unprofessionally. I'm not asking you to explain why almost every cop there was acting like they were guilty of something. All I'm asking is if either the phone or laptop has turned up."

She waited and could almost hear Burnside's brain working in the intervening silence.

"You didn't get this from me, okay?" he insisted.

"Of course not."

"Nothing's turned up on the laptop yet. We're still waiting. The phone is still missing too. But we traced it to its last known location, a few blocks away. We found the SIM card in an alley, or at least what was left of it. It had been crushed, and from the look of it, burned."

"That seems unusually thorough for a thief, don't you think?" Jessie noted. "Almost like the robber was more interested in keeping Michaela's call data hidden than in keeping her phone."

"I don't know what to tell you, Ms. Hunt," Burnside replied.

"No, of course you don't. As long as this conversation isn't officially happening, is there anything else you want to tell me about what occurred last night?"

More silence as Burnside weighed his response.

"I don't have anything more to share about last night," he finally said. "But I will say this. Going forward you might want to let this one go, Ms. Hunt. I can tell you don't want to. And I know from your reputation that letting things go isn't really what you do. But in this instance, you might want to reconsider."

"Why?"

"I have to go, Ms. Hunt. But I wish you all the best. Take care of yourself."

Before she could reply, he had hung up. She was pondering whether to call him back when she saw Garland Moses walk into the bullpen and make his way to the stairs leading to his tiny second-floor office. As usual, the legendary profiler projected the image of a rumpled, absent-minded professor, with his gray hair a mess, his glasses in danger of sliding off his nose, and his sport jacket dwarfing his wizened frame. She stood up and chased after him.

"Hey, Garland," she said, reaching him at the bottom of the stairs and walking up with him. "You'll never guess who I ran into yesterday."

"You shouldn't challenge me like that, Ms. Hunt," he replied, winking. "I guess stuff for a living, you know."

"Okay, then have at it," she teased.

"I'm going to say Dr. Janice Lemmon," he mused casually.

"How could you possibly know that?"

"That's easy. You know I know her and seemed delighted by that information when you found that out. Also, your current gossipy, schoolgirl tone suggests that whoever it is has what you believe to be some sort of personal connection to me. That limits the options pretty dramatically. Therefore, Dr. Lemmon."

"That's pretty impressive," she admitted.

"Also, she called me and warned me you were fishing for info," he said with a wink in his voice.

"I see," Jessie said, giddy at the thought. "Do the two of you chat on the phone often?"

"I feel like I've been transported into a Jane Austen novel and you're the scheming protagonist. Please tell me that you didn't accost me merely to hone your matchmaking skills, Ms. Hunt."

"That's not the *only* reason, Garland. I do have a favor to ask."

"What's that?" he said, as they reached the top of the stairs.

"I was hoping to introduce you to my half-sister, Hannah."

"Ah yes, the girl you saved from the serial killer."

"The girl you helped me save," Jessie corrected. "If not for your suggestion, I never would have found her."

"How is she?" he asked, brushing off the compliment.

"I was hoping you could tell me. I thought we could manufacture some sort of casual encounter and you could judge for yourself."

Garland looked at her disapprovingly as they approached his office door.

"So you want to introduce me to her under false pretenses so I can profile her because you're worried she might be a little serial killer-ish?"

"I wouldn't put it quite that way," Jessie protested. But . . . yes."

"I'm not totally comfortable with that," he told her as he opened the door. "I don't think it's fair to the girl and I worry that it might further erode the trust the two of you already sorely lack."

"How do you know tha..."

"However, I have to admit I'm curious to meet this girl. She sounds like a real pistol. I'd be willing to do that. To go through what she's suffered and still be even moderately functional? It's quite incredible. I can't guarantee anything beyond a chat. If you'll accept those terms, I'll agree to it."

"I'll take what I can get," Jessie said.

"Very well then. We can talk later to set something up," he said, then slammed the door in her face.

Under normal circumstances, Jessie would have been offended. But she decided to take the win. Garland had agreed to meet with Hannah. And once he did, Jessie was sure that he would be able to help. Even subconsciously, he'd end up profiling her. It was in his blood, just like it was in hers.

It was what they did.

CHAPTER EIGHT

By the time Ryan arrived, Jessie had a full head of steam. She'd spent the rest of the morning getting as much background information as she could on Michaela Penn. He had barely reached his desk before she started peppering him with details.

"Something doesn't fit with this girl," she said before he even sat down.

"Good morning, Jessie," he replied. "How are you?"

"Good morning," she said, offering a brief smile acknowledging the niceties of human interaction. "How am I? I'm confused. Michaela Penn is a real contradiction. This is a girl who graduated from a prestigious Catholic girls high school a year early while on an academic scholarship. She was legally emancipated at the age of sixteen. All very impressive, right?"

"Right," Ryan agreed, clearly giving up on the pleasantries.

"But the reason her emancipation was approved was because her father, who now lives up near Lake Arrowhead, was abusive. She was able to prove to the court that she was better off on her own."

"What about her mom?"

"Her mother died of ovarian cancer when she was seven."

"No other relatives?" Ryan asked.

"Not in California."

"Where did she live then?"

"Until she graduated early, she boarded at the school. Since then, she's bounced around among three different apartments until she settled on the place where she was found last night. None of the others were anywhere near as nice."

"So how did she afford the new place?" Ryan wondered.

"That's a good question. Like Lizzie said, she's a waitress. She works at Jerry's on Ventura Boulevard. And according to her manager, she only worked part-time. That's not going to pay for the place she was living in, much less all the art and electronics we saw."

"Any clues from her social media?" Ryan asked, finally firing up his computer.

"Not so far," Jessie admitted. "I've looked at her Facebook, Instagram, Twitter, Snapchat, WhatsApp, Tumblr, and Whisper accounts, along with everything else I could find. It's pretty standard stuff—selfies at the beach, pictures with friends at concerts, funny memes, inspirational quotes, tons of smiles; not a mean comment in her mentions. It's almost . . . too normal."

"What does that mean?"

"It's hard to explain. I know people's social media is curated to project the best possible image. But hers is relentlessly normal—nothing controversial, nothing revealing. It's just so impersonal. After looking at it all, I didn't get the sense that I knew her any better than before. It felt like a puzzle with several pieces missing."

"So there's nothing in there that would explain why someone would stab her multiple times?" Ryan asked drily.

"No," Jessie said, not playing along. "Nor why a bunch of cops would try to shut down the investigation before it began. By the way, I talked to Burnside earlier, the officer stationed outside the building last night. He basically begged me to drop the case. It sounded like he was genuinely concerned for me."

"Maybe he thinks Costabile is going to try to beat you up after school."

Before she could reply, Captain Decker poked his head out of his office and called them in.

"Hernandez, Hunt, I need to have a little chat, please."

Jessie glanced at Ryan, who had a look of resignation on his face.

"What?" she asked.

"That's his 'ream you out' voice," he said as he got up. "I can only imagine what the Valley Bureau people told him."

"Well, I've got a little reaming out of my own to do," Jessie said, her spine stiffening as she led the way to Decker's office.

"Great," she heard Ryan mutter quietly behind her. She pretended not to hear him.

They entered the office to find Captain Roy Decker standing behind his desk. He looked a decade older than his sixty years, skinny, mostly bald, and sunken-faced, with more wrinkles than she could count. He was staring at his computer screen with a frown. His beady eyes were intensely focused and his long, sharp nose seemed to point accusatorily in their direction.

"I understand you had a little excitement last night," he said without looking up.

"We stumbled onto a case with some unusual features," Ryan volunteered vaguely.

"Well, it seems that your involvement has piqued the interest of some of our friends in Valley Bureau," he replied, his voice betraying nothing.

Jessie wanted desperately to respond. But from experience, she'd found it best to let Ryan feel things out first. His many years of exemplary service had garnered him some goodwill that Jessie hadn't earned yet.

"Sir," Ryan began carefully, "I think their pique might have something to do with how they were caught flat-footed on this. They were violating protocols left and right. Hell, the body was being removed before the assigned detective had even arrived. It wasn't their finest moment."

"They neglected to include that in the preliminary report," Decker acknowledged. "May I ask what you were doing there in the first place? It's not exactly your jurisdiction."

"Was in the area after dinner and heard word of a victim who had been stabbed multiple times. I'm like a moth to a flame when it comes to that sort of thing and thought Hunt's insight could be valuable so I asked her to help out."

Decker glanced up at him. Jessie could tell he wasn't fooled by Ryan's incomplete, pronoun-averse answer. She thought this might be the moment when he pressed them on the nature of their relationship, which they'd been keeping under wraps. But he seemed to think better of it.

"Well, according to the report, it looks pretty open and shut; robbery gone wrong. So I guess we can move on without any unneeded friction between precincts."

"Actually, Captain," Jessie said, speaking for the first time, "I'm not sure it's as simple as that."

"Of course you're not," Decker said, seeming to sink even further into himself. "Go ahead, Hunt. Ruin my day."

"I don't mean to do that, sir," she said, trying to harness all the diplomacy she could muster. "But the scene doesn't support the theory that this is just a simple robbery gone wrong. Hardly anything was stolen. The SIM card in the phone, which *was* taken, was completely destroyed. The killer went into the bedroom with the murder weapon, seemingly with intent. The victim was stabbed nine times, hardly the MO of your typical apartment thief. And even after the girl was dead, the place was left largely untouched. I'm not saying definitively that it wasn't a robbery. But open and shut? I don't think so."

She wanted to go on; to say that something about the case stunk to high heaven. But deeming that extra claim to be counterproductive, she left it there.

Decker sat down and closed his eyes. When he opened his mouth, it was twisted into a pained grimace.

"What would you have me do with this information, Ms. Hunt?"

"Captain, I think you should allow us to pursue this case. Detective Hernandez's role as part of HSS allows him to take over any LAPD case the unit deems within its remit. Let us see where this goes. Give us the day. If we can't find anything worthwhile, we'll close up shop."

Decker sat quietly for a moment, weighing her proposition.

"Unfortunately, that's not possible," he said, turning to Ryan. "Detective Hernandez, I just got word that your testimony in the Barton murder case has been moved from tomorrow to today. You need to be at the courthouse at ten a.m."

Jessie and Ryan exchanged deflated looks.

"Captain," he pleaded, "it's only eight thirty now. Let me start the process of taking over the case. Maybe we can conduct an interview with the roommate. At least let us get the ball rolling."

"I can't do all that. I'm not going to pull the Valley guys off the case. The politics of that are just too ugly. But I can offer a compromise. I'll let Valley Bureau know that HSS wants to work in concurrence with them, to information share and pool resources. That will allow you access to witnesses and evidence."

"But we need to access all that now, sir," Jessie insisted, "while the trail is hot."

"Hunt, will you please let me finish before you dictate procedure to me?"

"Sorry, Captain," Jessie said, silently berating herself for alienating the man who could most help her out now.

"Hernandez, you put in the paperwork and note Hunt as the profiler on the case, which will permit witness interviews at the very least," he said, then turned to Jessie. "Hunt, that should allow you to re-interview the roommate. Once the door is cracked open, Valley won't be able to easily close it."

"Thank you, sir," Jessie said.

"Just don't go overboard, Hunt," Decker implored. "I know that's not easy for you. But stick to interviews, work that can be justified under the 'profiler' job description. You'll be solo for a while until Hernandez gets out of court. Without a cop to back you up, you need to tread more lightly. Are you familiar with that concept, Hunt?"

"Vaguely, sir," Jessie said, smiling. "Thank you."

"Please don't make me regret this," he said, almost begging.

Jessie answered as honestly as she could.

"I'll do my best."

CHAPTER NINE

Jessie was waiting in her hospital room when Lizzie woke up.

The girl looked around, clearly disoriented. Jessie got up and held a cup with a straw to her lips. She sucked down the water voraciously.

"Can you talk?" Jessie asked when Lizzie was through gulping.

"Where am I?" the girl asked hoarsely. "Who are you?"

"You're in Valley Presbyterian Hospital," Jessie told her patiently. "I'm Jessie Hunt with the Los Angeles Police Department. We met last night, though you were pretty drugged up at the time. Do you remember last night?"

At first Lizzie just looked confused. But then the memories seemed to flood back in. In an instant she grimaced and closed her eyes tight.

"I remember enough," she said quietly.

"Do you remember talking to me?"

"Not really."

"Okay, then let's start fresh. I'm sorry, but the questions I have to ask you are going to be difficult. But in order to find out what happened to Michaela..."

"Mick," Lizzie corrected. "She went by Mick."

"In order to find out what happened to Mick, I'm going to be blunt and I need you to be honest, okay? Don't try to protect her memory by keeping important details from me. Everything is going to come out eventually, so the sooner the better. Are we clear?"

Lizzie nodded.

"Okay, let's start with how you knew Mick."

"We went to high school together at St. Ursula Academy. She graduated a year early and we kind of lost touch. But we reconnected a few months ago. I go to school at Cal State Northridge and didn't want to live on campus. She had a new place and wanted a roommate for company. So I moved in."

"It's a pretty nice place," Jessie said gently. "You were able to afford it as a student?"

"I only paid a quarter of the rent, basically for the room. She footed the bill for everything else."

"*She* could afford that?"

"I guess so," Lizzie said unconvincingly.

Jessie decided to hold off before pressing on that point.

"So you've been roommates a few months now?" she asked.

"Uh-huh. Since last fall actually."

"And what were you doing last night before you came home?"

"I had a study session. I came home around nine forty-five. Mick gets up early for work lots of days so I tried to be quiet in case she was asleep."

"But . . ." Jessie pressed, sensing Lizzie wanted to say more.

"But I saw that her light was on. So I peeked in and . . ." She trailed off.

Jessie opted not to push on the details of a crime scene she'd seen herself. She didn't want Lizzie's emotions to overwhelm her and prevent her from providing other important details.

"I asked you this last night but you were a little out of it. Did Mick have a significant other?"

"No. She was single."

"What about an ex?" Jessie asked. "Maybe a relationship that ended badly?"

"She wasn't romantically involved with anyone the entire time I lived with her. She wanted to keep the focus on work. She was trying to build a nest egg."

"Waitressing at Jerry's?" Jessie asked incredulously.

Lizzie looked at her uncertainly, then glanced away.

"Can I get some more water, please?" she asked.

"Sure," Jessie said, refilling the cup and returning it to her.

After the girl took several more large gulps, Jessie tried again.

"Lizzie, do you remember what I said about being honest? How hiding things wouldn't help Mick?"

Lizzie nodded.

"I think we're at the point where you need to think about whether you're helping her right now. We both know you're not being totally straight with me. Why don't you tell me what you're holding back? It'll save me time that I can better use to catch her killer."

Lizzie stared at her with a mix of guilt and apprehension. Then she lowered her eyes. Jessie was just about to try again when the girl spoke.

"She wasn't just a waitress. She was there because she could work part time and set her hours. Mostly, though, it was so she could tell people that's what she did."

"It wasn't?"

"She made most of her money . . . acting."

"Okay," Jessie replied, sensing that word was carrying a lot of weight. "What kind of acting?"

"The adult kind," Lizzie answered heavily.

"She did porn?" Jessie asked, wanting to make sure they were on the same page.

Lizzie nodded her head.

"But she was underage," Jessie said. "You have to be eighteen to make those movies."

"She paid a lot of money to get decent fake papers. I doubt they would have been enough if she was applying to work at Google or Northrop Grumman or something. But the people she worked for weren't exactly sticklers. They asked for the paperwork. She gave it. They let her work."

"Was she popular, well-known?" Jessie asked, her head swimming at the possibility of thousands of viewers, all potential suspects.

"She wasn't a star or anything," Lizzie said. "She'd only made about a dozen movies so far. But she said they were planning to put her in a lot more. She said they liked her work ethic. She showed up on time. She'd work long hours. She was never high."

Jessie wondered about the professional environment in which those qualities were considered rarities.

"This was work she wanted to do?" Jessie asked.

"It wasn't her dream job. But she didn't have a problem with it. She liked to live on the edge a little, got a thrill out of being a bad girl. But mostly, she liked the money. She had a plan. She didn't live a fancy lifestyle. The apartment is nice and she generally bought what she wanted. But she didn't go crazy. She said that if she worked for two years and made fifty movies with multiple scenes—you get paid by the kind of act in each scene—she figured she could pull in about $250,000. Then she'd quit and go to school. She was looking into an advertising degree. She was already auditing my marketing class on Thursdays."

"Did she seem happy, like things were going okay?"

"I mean, happy is a strong word," Lizzie admitted. "She seemed okay with what she was doing. I tried not to press her on it too much. I don't like to judge but her lifestyle isn't my lifestyle. I'm pretty religious and she definitely wasn't. But considering that she was giving me such a deal on living there, I didn't think it was my place to call out her choices, you know?"

"I understand," Jessie assured her.

"It's not like she even needed a roommate really. She said she just felt more secure having one. And she liked the company. I think she appreciated having someone around who wasn't part of her work life, someone who knew her before she was Missy Mack."

"Missy Mack?"

"That's her screen name. She obviously wasn't going to use her real one. She said Missy sounded young and innocent, which is the type of character she was known for. Also it fit with her fake identity, Melissa Mackenzie. That was the name on the social security number she bought for employment documents."

"She really thought this through, huh?" Jessie said, half-admiringly.

"Like I said, she had a plan. Two years, $250,000. That was her focus."

"Was she working yesterday?"

"Yeah. She had an early call—six a.m. She was supposed to be there today too."

"Do you know the name of the company she worked for?"

"She did a lot of fly-by-night stuff for a while. But for the last half dozen movies, she's been a regular performer for Filthy Films. They're based here in Van Nuys."

Lizzie sighed deeply. Jessie could tell the girl was fading.

"Okay," Jessie said, writing it down. "I'm going to wrap up soon. Just a couple more questions—do you know if she had any obsessive fans? Did she ever mention stalkers or anything like that?"

"If she had any, she didn't mention them to me. You have to understand, we didn't really talk about what she did that much. She knew I wasn't super comfortable with it. And I think she just wanted to put it out of her head once she got home. So I doubt she would have brought up that kind of thing with me unless someone had done something really scary, like come to the apartment. We talked about movies, reality TV, friends from school. It never got too heavy."

A nurse walked in and, seeing Lizzie awake, immediately walked over to check her vitals.

"Am I going to be okay?" the girl asked.

"Yes," the nurse answered without hesitation. "You don't have any injuries. The EMTs brought you in because you were in shock. The doctor will do another evaluation. But I imagine you'll be able to leave in a few hours. Your recovery would be expedited by more rest and fewer disturbances."

Her last comment was accompanied by a raised eyebrow at Jessie, who had spent enough time recovering in hospitals under the care of protective nurses not to take offense.

"Last question and then I'll let you rest," she promised them both. "What do you know about Mick's father?"

Lizzie got quiet for a second. Clearly she knew something.

"She didn't talk about him much," she finally said. "And I only saw him once. He came to school one day at St. Ursula. He was stumbling around campus, really drunk, looking for her. He was calling out her name. You could hear it echo across the quad. The nuns had to call the cops."

"Did she ever talk about that incident or anything else related to him?"

"She just said that after her mom died, he started drinking a lot and got violent. I know he lives in some cabin in the mountains now and she seemed glad that he wasn't around."

The nurse gave an irritated grunt that indicated she was about to make a fuss. Jessie closed her notebook to prove she was done.

"Where will you stay?" she asked the girl. "How can I reach you if I have more questions?"

"My parents live in Thousand Oaks," Lizzie answered. "I'll probably crash with them for a while."

Jessie thought about how nice it must be to have the luxury to fall back on parents who would love and protect you when you were in crisis. It sounded like Michaela hadn't had that in a long time. Now that Jessie thought about it, neither did Hannah.

Neither did I.

CHAPTER TEN

Jessie felt dirty.

She had pulled over into a covered parking garage where she could take out her laptop and discreetly check out the work of Missy Mack. It didn't take long to find what she was looking for.

After randomly searching through a few film titles, she came across something called the Internet Adult Film Database. She punched "Missy Mack" into the search bar and a list of movies came back. She could quickly see what Lizzie had been talking about.

There were fourteen total films in her filmography. But the first few listed seemed to only include an individual scene with Missy. They also had bland names like *High School Gang Bang* and *BabeFest #29*. Each of those was made with a different production company.

It was only once she started working with Filthy Films that the creativity of the titles, and her total screen time, improved. The last six films on the list, all Filthy Films productions, included the likes of *Nympho Cheerleader Zombies*, *The Naughty Babysitters Club*, *Teacher's Pet*, and *Candy Wants Candy*, in which she seemed to be the main character.

It took some more digging to find the actual office address of the company and the real names of the people who ran it. But after some searching, with the assistance of the records team back at Central Station, she had a lead. As she pulled out of the garage and headed in that direction, she made a phone call.

Kat picked up on the second ring. Katherine "Kat" Gentry was one of Jessie's closest friends, which was odd, considering how they first met. Kat was the former head of security at the Non-Rehabilitative Division—NRD for short—of the psychiatric prison facility where Bolton Crutchfield was incarcerated. The two had initially butted heads when Jessie tried to interview the notorious serial killer as part of her thesis for her master's degree in Criminal Psychology.

Eventually the animosity faded as their mutual respect grew. Jessie revealed the truth about her childhood ordeal and her parentage. Kat shared details about her time as an Army Ranger in Afghanistan and the incident that led to the prominent scar on the left side of her face.

Somewhere along the line, a friendship blossomed. Then Crutchfield escaped. It didn't matter that Kat wasn't even in town when he broke out or that another security officer had secretly helped the killer. She got blamed and fired.

After taking some time off, she had recently recast herself as a private detective. Jessie tried to throw work her way as often as she could, partly out of friendship and partly because she felt responsible for what happened. Somewhere deep down, she'd always suspected that Crutchfield had escaped, at least in part, so he could better play his cat-and-mouse game with her.

"Hey. What's up?" Kat asked.

"Are you working any cases right now?" Jessie wanted to know.

"Nice to hear from you, Jessie. Hope you're well. I'm doing okay, thanks for asking."

"Sorry about that," Jessie said, chastened. "How are you?"

"I'm married now. Met a great guy. I was tailing him as a possible adulterer. But it turned out he was just a drug dealer. I was so impressed with his marital fidelity that I jumped him. He's leaving his wife for me."

"I said I was sorry," Jessie repeated. "Don't rub it in."

"I guess I forgive you. But maybe next time lead with the pleasantries."

"Noted," Jessie said, uncertain whether to proceed with her question.

"Okay," Kat said. "Now that you feel appropriately guilty, if you must know, I am between cases. I have a surveillance gig that starts this weekend. But right now, it's pretty quiet."

"Can I throw a job at you, one that I can't promise will be reimbursed by the fine folks at LAPD?"

"Jessie," Kat said patiently, "if I don't get paid, then that's what we call a 'favor,' not a job."

"You'll get paid one way or another. If they won't foot the bill, I will."

Kat didn't question the guarantee. She was well aware that as a result of Jessie's divorce from her wealthy but murderous husband, Kyle, she was financially secure enough to make such pledges.

"Now we're talking," Kat said with enthusiasm. "What can I do you for?"

"I want you to check into a guy named Keith Penn. He used to live in the San Fernando Valley but now he has a cabin in Lake Arrowhead."

"Sure. Want to give me the back story?"

"His daughter, Michaela, was murdered last night, stabbed nine times. She was only seventeen. Turns out she led a complicated life. I'm still trying to get a handle on it. But word is Keith was an abusive drunk. As a result, Michaela ended up getting emancipated."

"Sounds like a real charmer," Kat said. Between her time guarding serial killers and rapists and her stint in Afghanistan, she'd seen almost as much of the world's ugliness as Jessie had.

"I want to know what he was up to last night." Jessie told her. "Was he in his cabin? Did he make a visit to L.A.? Basically, I want a tick-tock on his movements for the last twenty-four hours. No need to confront him. I just need to know if he's a credible suspect."

"Are you leaning his way?" Kat asked.

"Too early to say," Jessie admitted. "But I really hope it's not him."

"Why?"

"Because Michaela was raped before she was murdered."

Kat was quiet for a moment. Even she couldn't be snarky about this.

"You know, we really must both be messed up people to do this kind of thing for a living. Have you ever thought of that?"

"Kat," Jessie replied. "Messed up is pretty much my defining characteristic."

Filthy Films really was filthy.

Or at least it was in a filthy location.

The company's production offices and studios were located in a rundown industrial part of Van Nuys. They shared the street with two bail bondsmen, a strip club, a liquor store, a payday lender, a smoke shop, and a security alarm store.

Jessie was reticent to park on the street and pulled up to the secured parking, where she flashed her LAPD badge to the security guard. It looked like a cop's ID save for the sticker at the bottom that said "profiler." Like almost everyone who glanced at it, he asked no questions and waved her through.

She parked and walked into the reception area where a woman in her sixties with thick bifocals sat behind a linoleum-topped counter. The woman looked up and peered at Jessie over her glasses. She had the craggy skin of someone who never bought into that whole sunscreen thing and was now paying the price.

"If you're here for the MILF auditions," she said in a cigarette-stained voice, "you're too late. They ended before lunch."

"I'm not here for the MILF auditions," Jessie said, unsure whether to be insulted or flattered.

"Good," the woman said. "You look too young anyway. Don't sell yourself short, dearie. You should come back next week. We're doing an open casting call for sexy teachers. We're starting a whole series. You're a better match for that."

"Thanks?" Jessie replied. "I'm actually not looking for work. I already have a gig with the LAPD. I'm looking for Leonard Lander."

The woman's eyes grew squinty and suspicious behind her glasses.

"What do you want with Lenny?"

"I need to ask him some questions regarding a case I'm investigating. I can't say more than that."

"Ugh," the woman said. "The first half-classy woman who wants to talk to my son in months and she's here to question him. Hold on."

As the woman picked up the phone, Jessie tried to decide which was more disturbing: that this woman worked at her son's porn company or that she considered Jessie to be "half-classy."

As they waited for him to answer, Jessie glanced at the posters on the walls of the office. Most appeared to be for titles from the Filthy Films catalogue— *The She-Wolf Chronicles, The Mile Higher Club, Mandy the Erotic Mermaid.* But mixed in were posters for *The Deer Hunter* and *Gandhi.* Jessie was flummoxed.

"Lenny," she heard the woman rasp, "it's Fiona. There's a police lady here to see you. She has some questions."

After a moment's silence, she spoke again.

"She won't give me any details. Just talk to her. You've got a scheduling meeting in ten minutes so this is a good window."

More listening.

"Yes, she's very nice-looking. But I don't think you'll have much luck, my sweet one. She looks like just being in here makes her want to bathe in Purell. Don't get your hopes up."

Still more silence, after which Fiona hung up.

"He'll be right up, dearie. Can I offer you something? Coffee? Seltzer? Hand sanitizer?"

For the first time since entering the office, Jessie smiled.

"I like you, Fiona."

"Of course you do. I'm very likable."

A second later Lenny Lander burst through the door. He was a sight to behold. Thirty-something, short, sweaty, and pale, with black hair plastered to his scalp and about thirty extra pounds, he looked more like a guy who spent most of his time in a basement than on a film set. He looked at Jessie with a mix of lasciviousness and apprehension.

"To what do I owe the honor?" he asked with ridiculous grandiosity.

"I'm Jessie Hunt. I consult for the LAPD. I need some info on one of your . . . actresses."

"Looking for a date?" Lenny asked, giving a broad, toothy smile.

Under normal circumstances, Jessie would have asked to speak to the guy privately. But somehow she suspected that would be counterproductive in this case. She might get more direct answers and fewer snarky comments if Fiona was around.

"This isn't a joke, Mr. Lander," she said plainly. "And I suggest you stop treating it as such. I need to know everything you can tell me about the actress who goes by the name Missy Mack."

Lenny looked only slightly tempered.

"Missy? The first thing I can tell you is she didn't show up this morning, which really screwed up my day. I had to find a replacement girl on short notice and shoot out of sequence. It probably cost me close to eighteen hundred bucks."

"Is that a common problem with her?" Jessie asked, deciding to hold back the reason for her absence for now.

"No. That's why it chapped my ass so much. She's usually on time and ready to go. I always have a girl on standby in case of no-shows. But with

Melissa—that's her real name—I got lulled into complacency because she never missed a call. So I skipped the standby this week. I should've known better."

"Usually she was more professional?" Jessie asked.

"For sure," Lenny said. "You know baseball?"

"I guess," Jessie said, curious where this analogy was headed.

"Well, she's like a five-tool player," he said enthusiastically. "She can play the seductress or be demure. She knows her lines. She hits her marks. She doesn't complain. She's up for anything, if you know what I mean. I guess that's more of a six-tool player. Seven if you actually count tools."

Lenny chuckled at his own joke. Fiona groaned quietly.

"Was she having any issues with anyone working on the film?" Jessie continued, pretending not to have heard that last line. "Professional dispute? Personal beef?"

"Why?" Fiona asked, clearly more concerned than her son. "Did something happen to Melissa?"

Jessie didn't feel like she could evade the question any longer without drawing suspicion so she decided to tell the truth.

Ideally she would have had someone else with her to give the news so she could observe their responses. Ryan usually played that role. But since she was alone, she kept her focus on Lenny, who seemed a more likely potential suspect.

"Melissa was murdered last night."

CHAPTER ELEVEN

"Oh my god," Fiona exclaimed.

"What?" Lenny asked, apparently not totally processing the news. He looked confused by her words.

"She was found in her apartment by her roommate," Jessie said. "We're investigating what happened. So you can understand that learning about any potential issues she had on-set or with a co-worker is essential to finding out what happened."

"This can't be right. I just saw her," Lenny said, still not grasping things completely.

"When was that?" Jessie asked.

Lenny looked over at his mother helplessly. Fiona pulled up a screen on her computer.

"Yesterday we wrapped for the day at five eighteen," she said, studying the screen. "She would have gone to makeup after that. Getting back to an everyday look is an involved process. Unless a girl has a public event or is doing a set at a club afterward, she'll usually want to peel everything off. Same with wardrobe—most of our girls like to leave here makeup free and in sweats so don't they draw ... unwanted attention."

"Stalkers?" Jessie asked.

"More just overenthusiastic fans," Fiona said. "But it can be a lot. None of them want to be hit on at the local Starbucks. I'm sure you get the same thing, dearie. For a lot of the girls, going without makeup is a kind of disguise because they look so different."

"You say she would have gone to wardrobe too. Was she a cheerleader for this movie?"

Lenny seemed to snap out of it slightly at the question.

"Yeah. We were shooting *Nympho Cheerleader Zombies 2.* The original was one of our biggest hits."

"She was found in her cheerleader uniform," Jessie said, ignoring his box office commentary. "How unusual would it be for her to wear her costume home?"

"A little," Fiona said. "But it's not crazy. That's a simple uniform to prep. If she kept it, she probably could have slept an extra half hour this morning. Normally the wardrobe girls have to find the outfit, check it out, and dress her. She could have just shown up in it and had wardrobe do a quick check. The head costumer doesn't like that in general because of potential damage. But because it was Melissa, I bet she would have let it slide. It's not like we're doing *Shakespeare in Love* here."

"Yeah," Jessie said. "It seems like a lot of what goes on here wouldn't pass muster in the normal film world."

"What's that supposed to mean?" Lenny demanded, looking offended. "We follow all the industry standards. We wipe down facilities after every scene. We haven't had a health shutdown in over three years."

"That's very impressive," Jessie said, trying not to gag. "But what about following employment rules?"

Lenny looked over at his mom like a kid who was worried he might get busted for stealing a cookie. Fiona sighed.

"We follow standard procedure," she said. 'Everyone needs to provide the same paperwork they would to work at a grocery store or at a shop in the mall."

"It looks like your age verification procedures could use a little brushing up," Jessie said.

"What do you mean?" Fiona asked as she punched the keyboard in front of her. "I'm looking at her file now. Everything is in order."

"Melissa was seventeen," Jessie told her. "And her real name isn't Melissa Mackenzie. It's Michaela Penn."

"What the . . .?" Lenny started to say.

"That's not possible," Fiona said. "I'm looking at copies of her documents right here—license, social security card—they're legit."

"A basic background check would have told you that the Melissa Mackenzie with that social security number died as a baby eighteen years ago. It took me two minutes to confirm it."

"But you're a cop," Fiona protested.

"You don't have to be a cop to verify this information," Jessie said, not correcting the woman's misimpression about her profession. "It's easy to confirm. I suspect that age verification just isn't a priority for Filthy Films."

"Listen," Lenny insisted. "We follow the rules. Missy, Michaela, whoever she is, was trumpeted by Giles. He pushed for her. If there was anything sketchy about her background, he's the one who should have known."

"Who's Giles?" Jessie asked.

"Giles Marchand," Fiona said. "He's one of our top directors. He did the original *Nympho Cheerleader Zombies.* He kind of discovered Melissa. He's been known to push hard for girls he likes. Last year he got a girl cast on *Nasty Maids Make a Mess* who turned out to be undocumented. He helped her get papers to suggest otherwise. But she was an idiot and started bragging about how her 'precious Giles' made her an American. Another girl who wanted her role turned her in. I wouldn't be stunned if he did something similar for Mel . . . Michaela."

"Can you please ask him to come here so we can talk?" Jessie asked.

"He's actually at home," Fiona said. "We wrapped early today and he's reviewing footage in the edit bay he has set up at his place."

"I'll go there then," Jessie said brusquely. "I need his contact info."

As Fiona looked it up, Lenny sat down on the worn, discolored loveseat in the corner of the office.

"I can't believe Missy's dead," he said foggily. "I had big plans for her. She was going to be the tent pole character for the *Candy Wants Candy* series. The second one is coming out next month. I guess now we'll just have to hype it as the last great performance of a talent cut down too soon."

Jessie was amazed and horrified at how quickly Lenny seemed to transition into thinking of how to monetize the death of one of his actresses. She felt anger bubble up in her chest and forced herself to gulp it back down before she spoke. She waited until Fiona handed her Giles's info before responding.

"You should know I'm having you shut down," she said to Lenny coldly. "Whether you were aware of it or not, you employed an underage girl in multiple porn films. That's not going to fly. So I wouldn't go making any elaborate marketing plans for her movies anytime soon. I have a feeling the FBI might take issue with that."

"But we'll lose hundreds of thousands of . . ."

But before Lenny could continue, Fiona shushed him. She seemed to sense that protesting would only make things worse.

"Thanks for bringing this to our attention," she said through gritted teeth. "We'll do everything we can on our end to help."

Jessie gave her a perfunctory nod and walked out, happy to let mother and son hash out the fallout without her.

Chapter Twelve

On her way to see Giles Marchand, Jessie saw that she had missed a text from Kat that read simply "Update. Call me." She called her back immediately.

"That was fast," she said when her friend picked up.

"You're surprised? I'm good at what I do."

"Prove it," Jessie challenged. "What did you find out?"

Kat chuckled at the faux animosity which would have been real only two years prior.

"A local deputy up in Lake Arrowhead named Connor was familiar with Keith Penn. He offered to go check out the guy's cabin personally for me."

"That was nice of him."

"Wasn't it?" Kat agreed. "I may have given him the impression that I'd let him teach me to ski the next time I go up there."

"Small price to pay," Jessie said. "What did he learn?"

"He said it looks like Penn hasn't been at his cabin in days. His mail has piled up in his mailbox, his truck isn't there, and there are no tire marks since the last snow, which was two days ago. He also checked around town at his usual haunts, which he said essentially means local bars. It's Tuesday now and no one has seen him since before the weekend. He warned me that none of this was that unusual. Apparently when the guy goes on a bender, he'll often go off the grid too. Still, Deputy Connor was going to see if he could trace the guy's cell phone."

"This is not what I was hoping to hear," Jessie admitted. "I wanted to rule this guy out."

"Hold on, Jessie," Kat said. "I'm getting a call. It looks like it's my guy. I'll be right back."

While Jessie waited for her friend to get back on the line, she checked how far she was from Giles Marchand's house. The director lived in the hills of Sherman Oaks, about fifteen minutes from the Filthy Films offices. Parts of the neighborhood were run down. But Marchand lived in a ritzier section with a view of the whole San Fernando Valley.

"Jessie," Kat said excitedly, coming back on the line, "I've got news."

"I'm ready," Jessie said.

"You're not going to believe this but Deputy Connor got a hit on Penn's phone."

"Where is he?"

"He's in L.A. Specifically at the local Van Nuys jail. He was arrested early this morning on a DUI. According to Mitch, the folks there don't even realize the connection yet. I asked him not to clear that up just yet. I figured you'd want the first shot at him."

"Thanks, Kat," Jessie said. "It sounds like that deputy, or is it Mitch now, really earned a tutoring session."

"I agree," Kat said. "I looked up his photo on the San Bernardino Sheriff's Department website. He's pretty cute, maybe a little young."

"Just make sure he's at least eighteen," Jessie said drily.

"Thanks for the pro tip," Kat said. "He's still on the other line so I'm going to go."

She was gone before Jessie could reply. She was already winding her way up the hill on Beverly Glen Boulevard, almost halfway to Marchand's place. But she pulled over anyway. The director would have to wait. If the Valley Bureau cops got to Keith Penn before she did, who knows what nefarious trouble they'd cause? With that in mind, she made a U-turn and headed back down the hill.

Walking into the Van Nuys jail felt like entering the lion's den.

As Jessie made her way from the main reception area down the hallway that led to the holding cells, she kept an eye out for anyone from yesterday evening. She kept reminding herself that they would all likely be off duty right now since most of them worked through the night.

When she got to the sign-in desk to see inmates, she had a half-second of panic. She was required to check in via computer rather than scratch her name on a sheet. That would put her on the radar. If anyone here cared to track her official whereabouts, then her current location would show up immediately.

Normally she wouldn't care. But after last night's combative interactions and Officer Burnside's cryptic warning this morning, she couldn't help but worry that her presence here might cause some curiosity or worse among Valley Bureau law enforcement. She'd have to move quickly.

Once signed in, she hurried to the visitor meeting waiting area. In the next room, she could see inmates talking to guests through glass partitions on corded wall phones. It took about five minutes for Keith Penn to be brought in.

She knew it was him even before she was told to meet him at window four. The man, who looked to be in his early forties, shuffled to the window slowly, as if he worried that taking full strides might lead him to fall over. His graying black hair was poking in every direction. He had a good four days' worth of stubble and though the sclera of his eyes was more red than white, they were otherwise the same as Michaela's. As he eased himself into the chair, almost missing it, Jessie realized he was still drunk.

She walked over, sat down across from him, and picked up the phone. He just stared at her so she motioned for him to do the same. He looked confused but did as she instructed.

"Mr. Penn," she said when he put the phone to his ear, "my name's Jessie Hunt. I consult for the LAPD. I was hoping you could answer a few questions for me."

"Is this about Michaela?" he asked.

"Why do you ask that?" Jessie asked, surprised.

"Because no one will tell me anything. No one even cares."

"What do you mean?" she pressed, increasingly confused.

"I've been trying to find out what happened to my baby for hours now but no one has told me anything since that first cop."

"What first cop?"

"I can't remember his name," Penn said, mumbling. "Constant or something. He called me last night and said my daughter had been killed in a robbery and that they would release her remains to me today. I thought someone was screwing with me so I hung up. But he called back and said it was true."

"He just told you flat out like that?" Jessie asked, horrified.

"Yeah," he said, his voice disconnected and flat. "He said they had positively identified her. He said I should come to the station and someone would take me to the morgue. So I drove down. But I got picked up when I got here and thrown in jail."

"Picked up?"

He sighed deeply, as if telling this story was physically intimidating.

"Yeah," he finally said. "You see, I was real upset. So I stopped off on the way down here—I live up in the mountains—for a drink to take the edge off. You know, in her honor."

"Which was it?" Jessie asked, knowing she shouldn't bait him but unable to stop herself. "To take the edge off or in her honor?"

Penn looked at her blankly, still too soused to be offended by the edge in her voice.

"Both. Anyway, one drink turned into two and I guess I lost control a little. But when I left, I came straight to Van Nuys. That's when I got pulled over. I told them why I was here. But I couldn't remember the name of the cop who called me and they didn't care anyway. They just booked me and threw me in the cell. You're the first person I've gotten to actually talk to me since then."

"Mr. Penn, I just want to make sure that I'm understanding all this correctly. You're saying that you were in Lake Arrowhead last night when you got a call from a Van Nuys police officer telling you that your daughter was murdered and you should come here. You left your home and drove here through the night, stopping at a bar for several drinks. Then you continued to Van Nuys, where you were picked up for drunk driving and taken here, where you've been held until now. Do I have all that right?"

"Mostly," he said, his voice thick and slurry.

"What did I get wrong?"

"I didn't come here from my place. I spent the weekend crashed at my buddy's in Running Springs. But other than that, you got it."

"You spent the last few days at a friend's place?"

"Yeah. We were hunting and fishing and drinking and stuff."

"Your buddy can confirm all this?" Jessie pressed.

"Sure. He's actually kind of pissed 'cause I messed myself a bit in his extra bed."

"I'll need his contact information," Jessie said.

"His name's Buck Crowder. I don't remember his number but it's in my phone if you look. If you get me out of here I can show you."

"I don't think they're going to let you out to show me, Mr. Penn. But I'll look into it. Let me ask you just a few more questions. The officer who called you with the news about Michaela—was his name possibly Costabile?"

"That sounds right," Penn said, nodding.

"And he said they would release her remains to you today?"

"Yeah. Why?"

"Did he say what would happen to them if you weren't available to collect them?"

"That they'd be disposed of."

Jessie's mind began to race. She wasn't sure how long she sat there silently until Penn interrupted her thoughts.

"What is it?" he asked.

She jumped slightly.

"Nothing," she said quickly. "I'm sorry for your loss, Mr. Penn."

She stood up and hung up the phone, trying to look calmer than she felt. As she walked out of the holding area, one question consumed her.

What exactly are these cops hiding?

She was poring over the possibilities in her head when she rounded the corner and bumped into the one person she didn't want to see: Sergeant Hank Costabile.

Chapter Thirteen

"What a pleasant surprise," Costabile said, his voice dripping with sarcasm as they disentangled themselves. "Slumming it?"

Jessie did her best to hide her discomfort but knew that he'd likely seen a flash of anxiety cross her face. Up close in the full light of day, the guy was even more imposing than he seemed last night. He was clearly a weightlifting fan, with thick, muscled biceps and forearms and a neck like a small tree trunk. His slight paunch was masked by his massive chest, which seemed to jut forward independent of the rest of his body.

"Just following up on a lead," she said vaguely, though she was certain he knew why she was here.

"Oh yeah?" he asked with malicious glee. "Is your lead sober yet?"

Jessie knew guys like this. As much as he was enjoying screwing with her, he was also trying to keep her off balance so that she wouldn't focus on whatever it was he was clearly hiding. She decided her best option was to be equally as aggressive.

"Let me ask you a question, Sergeant. What would happen if a relative failed to claim the body of their deceased loved one after being notified of the death?"

Costabile smiled malevolently.

"That would depend on the particular circumstances, Ms. Hunt. Unfortunately, if you're referring to the case from last night, there was an unfortunate mishap."

Jessie's heart sank, though she wasn't surprised. The second Keith Penn had mentioned claiming Michaela's remains, she'd suspected something sketchy was going on.

"What was that?" she asked.

"It seems that the paperwork on Michaela Penn got misfiled and her remains were inadvertently cremated."

Jessie stared hard at him. Even having suspected what he'd been about to say, it was hard to keep the fury off her face. She took a long, slow exhale before responding.

"That is unfortunate," she replied evenly. "Under other circumstances, I'd find cremating the body of a murder victim less than twenty-four hours after her death to be suspicious. But I guess that's just par for the course for Valley Bureau, right? Always bumbling and stumbling your way through major cases."

"Yup," Costabile agreed, his bald pate gleaming under the fluorescent lights. "We're just a bunch of Keystone Cops around here. I was just going to share the sad news with Mr. Penn, who I understand was picked up on a DUI in our own jurisdiction last night. What a wacky coincidence."

Jessie remembered the old cliché about discretion being the better part of valor and tried to force herself to embrace it. If Ryan was here right now, he'd make a bland comment and lead her out of the station before she could get herself in trouble. But Ryan was in a downtown courtroom right now testifying in a case. She was on her own. And she wasn't feeling much in the way of discretion.

"You know, Sergeant," she growled as she leaned in close to him. "I know you're up to no good, mostly because you're barely even trying to hide it. And I know you've had free rein around here for a long time. But it's made you sloppy and arrogant. One of these days, it's going to catch up to you, maybe sooner than you think."

"Is that a threat, Ms. Hunt?" he snarled back at her.

"It's merely an observation, Sergeant."

Suddenly Costabile leaned in, so that his face was only inches from hers.

"You know, little lass," he whispered so quietly that she had to strain to hear him, "if I was you, I'd be less worried about what some Podunk Valley cop was up to. I'd be more focused on watching your own back."

"Is *that* a threat, Sergeant Costabile?" Jessie retorted.

"Yes, it is. Go back to your fancy downtown station and stick to your sexy serial killer cases. It's safer for you than messing with me."

Jessie's heart was beating fast but her voice was calm when she replied.

"I'm glad we understand each other," she said.

Then, without waiting for a response, she spun on her heel and walked away. It was only when she had rounded the corner that she realized she'd been holding her breath the whole time.

Jessie tried not to speed.

She kept having to remind herself not to floor the accelerator on her drive back up the winding road to the home of the porn director Giles Marchand. But her restlessness kept getting the better of her. There was too much to do and not enough time to do it.

She still had to question the director of *Nympho Cheerleader Zombies 2* to see what insight he could offer into Michaela's last day alive. In addition, she was flying through a flurry of calls.

The first was to the tech unit back at Central Station to have them check the GPS data on Keith Penn's phone. If they could verify that he was traveling from Running Springs to Van Nuys, with an extended pit stop at a roadside bar, it would form the basis of a credible alibi.

Next she called Ryan, hoping he might be on a break from the trial. But her call went straight to voicemail. She briefly updated him on recent details, including Michaela's cremation, her dad's DUI, arrest, and possible alibi, and Sergeant Costabile's overtly suspicious behavior.

When she hung up, she saw that she'd missed a call from an unfamiliar number while she was leaving the message. She immediately played it.

"Hi, Ms. Hunt, this is Detective Wiley Strode of Valley Bureau, Van Nuys Station. I'm assigned to the Michaela Penn case. I understand that Detective Hernandez with HSS has filed to work concurrently on the case and that you both were at the crime scene last night before I arrived. I've been trying to reach him all day without success so I thought I'd reach out to you to coordinate our resources. Unfortunately, there doesn't seem to be much to coordinate. It's increasingly looking like this case may end up in our unsolved file. Regardless, please give me a call when you get a chance to compare notes."

Detective Strode's tone was professional and courteous and, at least on the surface, it seemed like he wanted to cooperate. But underneath the pleasant demeanor, it was clear that his bottom line wasn't much different than Sergeant Costabile's.

As far as he was concerned, the investigation was closer to the end than the beginning, a strange attitude to have when it came to the brutal stabbing murder of a teenage girl. No one at Valley Bureau seemed to care much about solving this case. In fact, they all seemed actively invested in *not* solving it.

The last concern gave her an idea and led her to immediately make another call. Again, she got voicemail, this time for Garland Moses. She tried to keep her message brief.

"Garland, you're pretty old," she began, hoping to soften her request with some disarming humor. "I'm hoping that since you've been around the department for so long, you might be able to give me some insight into some Valley Bureau personnel, specifically at Van Nuys Station. One is Detective Wiley Strode. But I'm especially interested in an officer named Sergeant Hank Costabile. He's inserted himself into a case I'm pursuing in some really intrusive, borderline threatening ways. Have you heard of him? If so, what can you tell me? If not, can you work your 'on the sly' magic and get me some intel? I know the guy is bad news but I'm flying blind about just how bad. Thanks in advance."

She hung up, uncertain if she was abusing the veteran profiler's generosity with the request. But she knew there was no way she was going to smash through the blue wall of silence through conventional means. Even Ryan, who'd been a cop for a nearly a decade, seemed only to have a general sense of Costabile. She needed help from someone who'd been around the department much longer than that.

Her last call before pulling up at Marchand's house was to Detective Gaylene Parker in Vice. She told Parker about Filthy Films using an underage actress and asked who she needed to contact to get something done about it. Parker, who sounded personally offended, said that she would call the right people and guaranteed that all Filthy productions would be shut down by the end of the day.

With that off her plate, Jessie focused on the task at hand. She got out of her car and walked up Marchand's circular driveway to the front door. While his house was large and had a hilltop view of the currently hazy valley, it was dated, with seventies-style ranch house architecture and a few dangling shingles. It looked like a fixer-upper that had never been fixed up.

I guess porn directing isn't the cash cow I assumed it was.

She rang the bell and waited, curious to meet the creative mind behind some of the works she'd surreptitiously watched on her laptop earlier. When Giles Marchand opened the door, she had to stifle a gasp.

CHAPTER FOURTEEN

Jessie forced herself to cough to hide the snort of laughter she feared might escape her mouth.

The man was a walking cliché. He appeared to be in his mid-fifties and though he may have cut a dashing figure at one time, now he looked like a guy clinging to past glory. His salt and pepper hairpiece was too lustrous to look real and the line where it met his more straw-like, real hair was distinct.

He was over-tanned, with deep, olive skin that covered every exposed inch, including, disturbingly, directly under his eyes. His teeth were unnaturally white and appeared to have been surgically altered to look more square. He was clearly an aficionado of Botox and had over-dimpled cheeks and a forehead suspiciously devoid of wrinkles. Finally, his oddly formal posture made Jessie wonder whether he might be wearing a girdle of some kind.

"I swear I'm not the father," he said with booming, overly-familiar jocularity.

For a second, Jessie was so stunned, she didn't know how to respond.

"Mr. Marchand," she finally managed to say, "my name is Jessie Hunt..."

"Paternity lawyer or aspiring actress?" he asked in a richly honeyed, clearly practiced voice, a broad smile on his face. Apparently he was fine with her being either.

"LAPD, actually," she replied, managing to regain some semblance of control over herself.

"Oh, that's new," he said, still unruffled. "You've piqued my interest. Care to come in? I can offer you some peppermint-cayenne tea and we can discuss whatever exciting development has brought you to my door."

"Thank you," Jessie said, stepping inside while eyeing him curiously. "I'll pass on the tea. But I'll happily get your answer as to why you're pretending you don't know the reason I'm here."

Marchand couldn't hide his surprise.

"Am I that transparent?" he asked, unashamedly.

"Yes," Jessie said. "Also, there's no way Lenny Lander didn't call you the second I left his office."

"Now that you mention it, Ms. Hunt," he said as he led her into the living room, "I did get a call a little while ago from Leonard. He was most disconcerted by your visit. Truthfully, despite my brave front right now, I spent much of the last few hours shedding internal tears over the loss of dear Missy."

"Internal tears?" Jessie repeated.

"Yes, darling. I've had some work done and I've largely lost the capacity for crying; a blessing and a curse."

"I see. And you know that Missy wasn't who she said she was?"

"Fiona told me that she was operating under a false name. I never called her Melissa anyway. I only ever address my actresses by their stage names. It's a small thing, but I find that it helps them stay in character."

As best she could, Jessie tried to separate Marchand's ostentatious manner from the words he was saying. She found that it helped to focus on the man's nose, which seemed to be the one feature that hadn't had any work done on it.

"I noticed that you said Fiona told you about her fake name. But my understanding is that you have a history of helping some of these girls find those names. Isn't that true?"

"I'm not sure what you mean, Ms. Hunt," he said, though his expression suggested he knew exactly what she meant. His smile remained plastered on, but his eyes were less confident.

"Let's not be coy, Mr. Marchand. You have a reputation for getting fake papers for women you want in your films."

"Those are just vicious rumors," he insisted far too dramatically. "I would never do anything untoward. I only want what's best for my actresses. I saw a great future for Missy. I think she could have been one of the greats."

"Why is that?" Jessie asked, a little afraid to hear the answer, taking the bait though she knew he was deflecting.

Marchand's eyes gleamed with mischievous glee.

"Because she had that special 'thing.' Do you know what I mean?"

"I'm afraid I don't."

"She was magnetic on camera," he told her in a hushed whisper. "She pulled the viewer in. No matter what character she played—student seducing the teacher, girl who gets it on with her tutor, cheerleader with the football player, naughty babysitter—she was always compelling."

Jessie paused for a moment before replying to see if he noticed the similarity in those scenarios, but he seemed oblivious.

"Mr. Marchand," she said. "You do realize that every character you described her playing just now was a potentially underage girl."

"That was her thing," Marchand replied, untroubled. "She looked young so she was a natural for the 'barely legal' plots."

"But here's the problem, and I think you're well aware of it. Michaela Penn *wasn't* legal. She was seventeen and working with obviously false documentation."

Marchand stared at her with what he clearly hoped was shock.

"I find that hard to believe," he insisted. "Missy never gave off the vibe that she was seventeen. I would have guessed she was closer to twenty-one. She oozed maturity."

Jessie was impressed with Marchand's brazen willingness to pretend he was an innocent in this whole thing. But part of her wondered if a guy this willing to deny reality when confronted with it might be capable of emotionally disassociating himself from other, far darker behavior. She decided to switch tacks to see if she could rattle him.

"Did you and Michaela get along?" she asked.

"Magnificently," he said loudly, as if he were announcing it to a full theater. "We were absolutely simpatico. I don't want to sound arrogant here. But had this not happened, I feel like we might have become the Scorsese and De Niro of the adult market."

"That doesn't sound arrogant at all," Jessie observed drily, unable to help herself. "What about co-workers? Any jealous actresses who wanted her roles or scene partners she might have dated and then broken things off with?"

"I'm sure some of the other girls were jealous, but to the point of violence? I find that hard to believe. As for dating, Missy was known for her firm policy on that. She refused to get involved with anyone she worked with. In fact, I don't think she was seeing anyone at all. She was very focused on her career. There was no B.S. with that girl. She was all business."

After all Marchand's dissembling, this was the first thing he'd said that Jessie felt was completely genuine. His description of Michaela's work ethic and obvious admiration for it was clear. It also matched Lizzie's account.

"Where were you last night?" she asked, hoping that his honesty in his last answer might bleed over into this one.

"Is this the part where I provide my alibi?" he asked, rediscovering his arch tone.

"It is."

"Well, after Leonard called, I thought I might be asked this, so I reconstructed a timeline of my whereabouts after I left the set yesterday afternoon. First I went to dinner with one of our fine performers—her name is Melanie Mynx—to give her some professional pointers. Her onscreen enthusiasm has been proving a little histrionic. It doesn't have the ring of truth. So we did some scene analysis."

"And then?" Jessie prodded, fearing he would get into specifics of the analysis.

After that, we went to a house party in Toluca Lake, where I introduced her to some other friends. We spent some 'quality time' there. If you're wondering, I'm being euphemistic. We had an orgy. I can give you the names and contact information for all of those people. Then Melanie and I went back to her place, where she hosted me for the remainder of the evening. This morning I came back here briefly to clean up before heading to set."

Jessie wanted to be suspicious about how meticulously Marchand had accounted for his time. But it struck her as fitting his personality. Still, she prodded a little, watching closely for his reaction to the next question.

"Are you sure Melanie was awake for the whole evening?" she asked him. "Maybe she fell asleep for a stretch there?"

"Are you alleging that while she slept, I snuck out of her apartment, murdered my rising star actress, and then returned to Melanie's bed?" he asked, his eyebrows raised as high as they could go given the Botox.

"It's just a question, Mr. Marchand—one I noticed you neglected to answer."

"I'll answer. I was just so taken aback at the suggestion. I spent the entire evening in the loving embrace of Ms. Mynx. Okay, loving might be overstating it. If you want, I can offer details on the nature of the embrace, but you strike me as the type who might blush at such things."

"I have your answer," Jessie replied, though not to his dig. "My team will verify it. In the meantime, I recommend you stay in town. And you may want to eat at home a little more often. I have a feeling your production schedule is going to grind to a halt very soon."

"What?" he asked, his jaw dropping precipitously.

Though she didn't smile, Jessie felt a sense of satisfaction for the first time in her interaction with this guy.

"I appreciate the whole dandy thing, Mr. Marchand," as she headed for the door. "But if you think roguish, old-school, smarmy charm is going to allow you to use underage girls in your films, you are sorely mistaken. So I recommend you and your closet full of ascots make alternate plans for the next few months because business is about to dry up."

Though it was incredibly tempting, she didn't look back as she walked out and closed the front door behind her. Unfortunately, the high was short-lived. By the time she got to her car, she remembered that she was no closer to finding Michaela's killer.

CHAPTER FIFTEEN

Jessie tried to keep the laptop's volume down.

Hannah was in the next room and she didn't want her teenage half-sister to hear the grunts and moans and wonder what she was watching. Normally, she wouldn't be watching porn in her bedroom after work on a Tuesday evening. But she was at a loss as to how to proceed.

She still hadn't heard back from Ryan or Garland Moses about her concerns regarding how Valley Bureau was handling—more accurately, not handling—the case. And while Michaela seemed to have interacted with a bevy of sketchy people, none of them was an obvious suspect.

So she was reduced to watching some of the girl's films, in the hopes that seeing her alive might spark some moment of insight. But mostly, it was just depressing her.

It was only once she started watching that she realized that, despite having made over a dozen films, all of them were from the last six months. The idea that this was how Michaela had spent the majority of her days since school made Jessie feel hollow and sick at the same time.

The girl's manner only exacerbated that. Michaela had a different demeanor from all the other actresses in any of the films. The others were always animated, sometimes to the point of being over-the-top, much like she imagined Melanie Mynx probably was. There was lots of groaning and whispered dirty talk. Michaela didn't do any of that.

Her bearing, even in the middle of acts Jessie hadn't even conceived of, was detached, even aloof. In fact, that seemed to be her thing. As her prominence in the movies increased, a recurring theme developed. No matter what scenario she was in, she always seemed to play a version of the ice princess.

Invariably, her character was a cold, reticent, even haughty teen who seemed unimpressed and sometimes even bored by the strenuous sexual efforts of her partner, sometimes partners. Everyone she engaged with wanted to be the one to crack the code and get her to warm up. Almost always, when she consented to participate, she came across as deeply disappointed by those she dealt with, consistently underwhelmed by even the most elaborate erotic gymnastics.

Jessie had to admit it was magnetic. Even she found herself wondering whether this guy or girl or that particular position or maneuver would be the one to finally satisfy Missy Mack. In a strange way that Jessie didn't want to consider too deeply, it was almost as if the girl was retaining some semblance of personal power by refusing to show any enthusiasm about what she was doing. It was almost as if she was saying, "You can do these things to me, but know that I'm mostly humoring you. Your presence serves my purposes, but only barely."

Hey, maybe watching this crap is helping me get some insight into her mindset after all.

There was something else about Mick that Jessie noticed—something she couldn't quite put her finger on. It was only in a scene in which the girl lied to her parents on the phone about being at the library when she was really in the locker room with the star quarterback that it clicked for her. Mick reminded her of Hannah.

Not in the obvious ways. While she didn't know her half-sister's sexual history, she got a definite sense that the girl was fairly inexperienced. And of course both of them were seventeen. But it was their manner that was so similar.

They had the same body language—guarded and taut, as if they might make a break for it at any moment. The eyes of both girls went blank, almost dead, when faced with an unpleasant circumstance. Mick's eyes in all her sex scenes had the same disconnected look that Hannah's had when she was tuning Jessie out or leaving an appointment with Dr. Lemmon.

And even though Mick was "acting" when she lied to her parents about her whereabouts, her casual comfort while doing it was reminiscent of how easily Hannah seemed to tell falsehoods, almost as if she wasn't even aware that she was lying through her teeth.

Jessie decided she needed a break from the images on her screen and the concerns they were raising in her mind. She was just about to close her laptop entirely when she heard a voice behind her.

"Ryan not getting the job done for you?"

Jessie spun around, almost knocking the laptop to the floor. Hannah's head was poking through a crack in the door.

"I thought I locked that," she said, feeling her face redden.

"You did," Hannah said, smirking. "But your bedroom isn't exactly Fort Knox and I used to have overprotective parents. Considering that, you'd think I'd be the one shame-watching porn."

"It's actually for work," Jessie told her, fully aware how lame that sounded.

"Of course it is," Hannah said, her tone faux-sincere. "Are you about to go on some undercover operation?"

For half a second, Jessie considered fudging her answer. But then she realized that this might be a rare opportunity to connect.

"Actually, I'm investigating the death of the girl on the screen. She was murdered last night."

Hannah's smirk disappeared and she pushed the door open.

"Can I see her?" she asked.

Jessie nodded. Hannah came over and sat down on the bed beside her. She looked at the frozen image of Michaela, who was currently in a close-up, her expression one of mild interest in what was occurring off-camera.

"She looks young," Hannah said.

"She was. In fact, she was the same age as you. She had just graduated early from an all-girls Catholic high school. She lived in Van Nuys."

"St. Ursula, right?"

"Yes?" Jessie confirmed. "How did you know that?"

"That used to be my neck of the woods so it makes sense. What's her name?" Hannah asked, unable to tear her eyes away from the screen.

"Michaela Penn. But her friends called her Mick."

"She reminds me of girls I knew in school," Hannah said quietly.

That didn't shock Jessie. Her half-sister, until her life was upended, had gone to a private all-girls school in the Valley as well. On the surface, their lives probably weren't that different.

"I'm sure you can see some of yourself in her life," she agreed.

"No," Hannah said forcefully. "I mean, I know actual girls like her, who did porn on the side. I bet some of them knew her."

"You knew girls who did porn while attending your school?"

"A few," Hannah said. "I can think of at least five. Three had already graduated. One was a senior with me and one was a junior."

"There were that many girls at your school that did this?" Jessie asked incredulously.

"Yeah," Hannah replied, stunningly blasé about it. "In fact, some of them did more than that."

"What do you mean?" Jessie asked, though she suspected the answer.

"They would go on ... private dates to make extra money. At least a few of them did. I know the junior did for sure."

"So this junior girl who did porn and private dates—she was definitely underage," Jessie said.

Hannah rolled her eyes at the apparent naiveté of the question but managed to answer without sarcasm.

"I assume so. But I was only friendly with the one girl in my year. And she didn't really advertise it."

"Did she say why she did it?"

"We didn't ever talk about it," Hannah said. "But she was kind of wild— liked to party, liked to ... experiment."

"With drugs?" Jessie asked, trying not to sound too judgmental.

"Among other things," Hannah replied. "I also think her home life wasn't the greatest. She'd come to school with bruises sometimes and she'd occasionally talk about her dad being super-strict, like violently strict. I think this was her way of taking some control."

"That sounds familiar," Jessie mused. "Apparently Michaela didn't have the greatest home life either. Her mother died when she was younger and her father was an abusive alcoholic."

Hannah nodded.

"Sounds like she was a perfect candidate to end up doing what she did."

Jessie had about a dozen other questions she wanted to ask. But this was the first time in a while that Hannah had opened up about anything and she didn't want to scare her off or have her shut down. She forced herself to take a slow, calming breath.

But before she could speak again, her phone rang. She looked down. The call was from Officer Burnside.

"I have to take this. It's about the case," she told Hannah before she picked up. "This is Jessie Hunt."

"Ms. Hunt. It's Officer Burnside from last night."

"Hello, Officer," she said, keeping an even tone though she felt a sudden hit of adrenaline. "What can I do for you?"

"I can't talk for long. But I thought you should know there's been a hit on Michaela Penn's stolen laptop. It was just pawned at a shop on Victory Boulevard in North Hollywood."

"Is the seller still there?"

"No," Burnside said. "But the shop owner knows him—a guy named Pete Vasquez. Says he pawns stuff in there all the time. He also said Vasquez took the cash and immediately walked into the bar next door."

"Are your people en route?" Jessie asked anxiously.

"Not yet," Burnside said. "The owner called me directly because I helped him set up a security system after a robbery. I'm about to report it up the chain. But I decided to call you first. I'm not sure how it will go down when my station finds the guy. They're hyped to nail down a suspect so they can put this thing to bed."

"You think they might take him out and pin the murder on him?"

"I didn't say that," Burnside said emphatically. "I never said that."

"Okay," Jessie soothed. "I'm sorry."

"What I can say is that I looked at Vasquez's record. He's done some time but it's all for stuff like petty theft; never used a weapon, no violent crime. It's hard to see him as right for a stabbing murder."

"Okay, thanks, Burnside. How much of a head start can you give me? I'm downtown right now."

"Not too long. I'm going to the restroom because I think I'm suddenly developing some 'digestive issues.' I may be able to dawdle a little after that. But then it's going to look suspicious. Maybe twenty minutes?"

"I'll take it."

"I'll text you the address now," Burnside said. "And Ms. Hunt?"

"Yes?"

"Try to bring the detective from last night if you can. I don't know how this will go down and you may want some backup." Then he hung up.

With that warning still ringing in her ears, Jessie began scrambling around the apartment, grabbing essentials as she gave Hannah the basics.

"Do you know when you'll be back?" the girl asked.

"I don't," Jessie said as she threw on her jacket. "Your best bet is to finish any homework and expect to crash for the night while I'm still out. Sorry to bail but..."

"It's okay," Hannah said. "I understand."

Jessie gave her a quick smile before bolting out the door.

CHAPTER SIXTEEN

At times like this, Jessie wished she had a siren for her car.
Instead she had to rely on that old standby: speeding recklessly and hoping she didn't get pulled over. She was pulling onto the 110 freeway when she tried Ryan again. He picked up on the first ring.

"Sorry I haven't gotten back to you," he said before she could speak. "My phone died. I was testifying all day. I was meeting with prosecutors until just a few minutes ago."

"Don't worry about it," Jessie said. "Can you meet me in the Valley? There have been a few developments."

She explained the situation as she transferred onto the 101 freeway which cut through the Hollywood Hills along the Cahuenga Pass. She did her best to ignore the potholes on the decrepit stretch of road.

It was a lot for Ryan to take in but he seemed to process it all. When she was done, he offered what he admitted was limited insight.

"I don't know Detective Strode, never heard of him actually. That's not a great sign," he said. "Normally a murder like this gets assigned to the most experienced detectives in the Bureau. It's weird."

"It's more than just weird, Ryan," Jessie insisted. "It stinks. A police sergeant overtly threatens me. A murder victim is cremated before she can be autopsied. A rookie detective gets assigned to the case. Frankly, the question isn't if someone is being protected but how high up is that person? This can't all be Costabile, can it? He doesn't have *that* much pull."

"You're right, it does stink," Ryan agreed. "And this does seem to go higher than Costabile. But suspecting that doesn't change how we approach the case. We still have to grind out the work if we're going to unpeel what's really going on here. But there is one upside to having a rookie detective assigned to the case.

Because I'm representing HSS on this, I may be able to bigfoot him once I get there. Until then, you'll have to hold down the fort. How far out are you?"

"I'm probably still ten minutes away," she said.

"Okay. I'm about five behind you. Try not to get yourself shot before I catch up."

"Aw, so romantic," she replied before hanging up and immediately calling Garland Moses.

The elder profiler didn't pick up until the fourth ring and he sounded drowsy when he did.

"Ms. Hunt, have you ever heard the term 'elder abuse'? It's after ten p.m."

"I'm sorry, Garland. You know I wouldn't call at this hour unless it was pressing. Besides, I never heard back from you. I was a little worried."

"That's a lie," he said flatly, his drowsiness slipping away fast. "I'll let it go this time. But please, don't try to play me. I had every intention of getting back to you tomorrow. What is so pressing that it couldn't wait?"

Jessie decided not to linger on his accurate assertion that she was a liar and moved on to the issue at hand.

"I may be about to enter a hornet's nest in a few minutes and I really need your guidance. What can you tell me about Detective Wiley Strode and Sergeant Hank Costabile?"

She heard a bed creak and papers being shuffled and imagined him sitting up and putting on his glasses.

"I don't have much on Strode," he said, now sounding fully alert. "He was based out of Thousand Oaks until recently. He only just passed the detective exam last year and was reassigned to Valley Bureau. Until now, he's mostly been a robbery guy, a few home invasion cases. This is his first murder."

"That seems odd," Jessie said. "Wouldn't he normally get paired with someone more experienced, especially for a murder?"

"Normally? Yes. Of course, if there was a backload or major cases in the division, he might not."

"Do you know if there's a backload?" Jessie asked.

"I checked their case board earlier this evening. It's nothing out of the ordinary. In fact, there are two homicide detectives not currently assigned to any priority cases. And yet, Strode was put on this."

"What does that mean to you?" Jessie pressed.

Garland paused briefly before responding and she knew he was entering sensitive territory.

"There could be completely innocuous reasons for it that we're just not aware of," he began. "Or it could be an indication that someone with the power to influence case assignments wanted a less experienced detective on it or at least one with less pull in the Bureau. I tried to go through the paperwork to see who that might be. But the chain of command on this thing has been cleverly disguised. Your good friend Costabile's fingerprints are all over the place. But he couldn't authorize this kind of assignment shifting on his own. He'd have to be doing it on someone else's authority. And I can't discern who that might be."

"So this isn't all on Costabile?" Jessie asked.

"No. The guy's been around forever and amassed a lot of power among the rank and file. He also holds sway with the higher-ups in the Bureau and beyond. But the kind of things you're describing—assigning a rookie detective to a murder case, rushing a crime scene investigation, having a body 'accidentally' cremated—he can't make them happen on his own. He's getting help."

"Great," Jessie said, frustrated, as she pulled off the freeway onto Victory Boulevard. "So it could be anybody."

"That's not true," Garland said with a professorial tone. "It actually limits the number of candidates significantly. There are only so many people with both the authority to make those things happen and the ability to hide their involvement. You just have to find out who they are. But that leads me to one last thing."

"What's that?"

"You need to be very careful, Ms. Hunt. Whoever he's working for, Costabile is dangerous in his own right. The guy has a hair-trigger temper. He's been involved in multiple questionable shootings and never lost a day of pay. He has friends and lackeys everywhere. Don't underestimate him."

"Okay. Thanks for scaring the crap out of me, Garland."

"Better to be overprepared than taken by surprise. I know you've dealt with the worst the world has to offer—brutal serial killers. But a cop with power and ill intent is a different kind of dangerous. Just stay alert."

CHAPTER SEVENTEEN

Jessie was more hyper than alert.

When she pulled up near the Landing Strip, the bar on Victory where Pete Vasquez was supposedly holed up, she had to remind herself not to just barrel into the place.

The cops hadn't arrived yet so she tried to formulate a plan. Burnside had sent her a mug shot of Vasquez so she knew who she was looking for. Maybe she could sidle up to him and ask a few questions before he realized who he was dealing with. But that would require time to set him at ease—time she didn't have.

She decided to just go in and figure something out on the fly. As she opened her car door, she heard the sirens. For half a second, she considered sprinting into the bar before the police arrived and trying to whisk Vasquez away before they entered. But she knew the idea was ridiculous. Vasquez had no reason to go with her and she couldn't physically force him to.

It was moot anyway. A stream of black-and-white cars was already approaching in the distance. At this point, she'd never even get inside the club before they saw her. She closed the car door, quickly texted Ryan "Valley cops are arriving—stuck outside," and waited to see how it all played out.

Three squad cars and an unmarked sedan pulled up in front of the bar and everyone hopped out. Among them were Sergeant Costabile and a young-ish-looking man with short blond hair in plainclothes who she assumed was Detective Strode.

A patron loitering outside the front door saw them coming, yanked open the door, and ran inside. Even from across the street, Jessie could hear a voice shouting, "Pig raid! Pigs outside!"

The cops exchanged anxious looks and picked up the pace as all but one of them hurried inside. While the remaining officer stationed himself in front of the door, two additional squad cars sped down the street and screeched to a halt. Jessie watched them scramble out as well. Her attention was suddenly diverted by movement in the alley behind the bar.

Multiple people must have been escaping through the back exit. They were now racing through the alley back toward the main street. Unfortunately for them, the cops who had just arrived hadn't entered the bar yet and were standing on the sidewalk just in time to meet them.

"Freeze!" one of them shouted. "Everyone stay where you are with your hands up."

A few patrons who hadn't yet made it out of the alley to the front of the bar heard the instruction, stopped, spun around, and headed back in the direction they'd come. Just before he turned away from her, Jessie was able to see that one of them was Pete Vasquez. He rushed to the chain-link fence behind the bar. A few people were scaling it. He appeared to consider the idea before changing his mind and turning left down the alley that ran behind the strip center next to the bar.

Jessie turned on her engine and eased out onto the road, hoping not to draw the attention of the uniformed officers busy with the folks holding up their hands. One cop glanced in her direction but didn't seem interested in the worried-looking white woman trying to leave the scary scene. Jessie kept the concerned look on her face until she turned right onto Tujung Avenue. She pulled over to the side, turned off her headlights, and waited.

Only twenty seconds later, Vasquez came into view, walking briskly but "casually" down the alley, desperately trying not to look over his shoulder. The guy, who appeared to be in his mid-thirties, was clearly winded. He kept swiping his longish black hair out of his eyes and looked like he might trip over the cowboy boots he was wearing.

Jessie got out of her car and walked toward him, pretending to look at her phone but evaluating him as she moved. He was about five foot seven and a sloppy 180 pounds. She had him by three inches, and though he was a good forty pounds heavier than her, she doubted he knew how to effectively use it. She reminded herself not to underestimate him despite his unimposing appearance.

They were only about five feet apart when he finally seemed to notice her. She kept her head down, feigning obliviousness, and continued straight toward him. They were about to collide when he let out a "hey!" that she deliberately ignored, stumbling into him. She "accidentally" grabbed him for support, knocking him over as she "fell" to the ground.

"Sorry," she said apologetically as she offered a sheepish smile and put her phone in her pocket. "I wasn't looking where I was going. Are you okay?"

She popped up quickly and offered her hand to him. He looked like he had been weighing whether or not to yell at her. He was obviously pissed but didn't seem to want to attract attention.

"Yeah, I'm good," he finally said, apparently choosing discretion as he extended his hand. "Don't worry about it."

"Thanks," she said as she pulled him up. "Pete, is it?"

His eyes widened in surprise at the sound of his name and Jessie had her semi-official confirmation that she had the right guy. She wrenched her hand loose from his and he fell back, his butt landing hard on the concrete. Before he had time to do anything other than grunt, she'd pulled out her weapon and had it aimed directly at him.

"Hi, Pete," she said calmly. "My name's Jessie Hunt. I work for the LAPD. And I need you stick around. I have a few questions for you."

In the distance, she saw several cops burst out of the back entrance of the Landing Strip. Her breathing suddenly quickened. She guessed she had less than a minute before they saw her with Vasquez and ran over.

"Whatever it is, I don't know anything," Vasquez spat belligerently.

"Pete, I don't think you understand the serious situation you're in. Time is short so I can only explain this once. I'm investigating the murder of a teenage girl. She was stabbed to death last night. You just pawned her laptop a few doors down. That makes you the most likely suspect. In about forty-five seconds, the cops who busted into the bar are going to arrest you for that murder. I can't help you after that. But right now I can."

"How?" he asked, all trace of obstinacy gone as he looked back down the alley and saw the same thing she'd already noticed: three men in uniform charging toward them.

"I'm willing to give you the benefit of the doubt that you didn't kill her. But I need to know how you got that laptop."

"What about my Miranda rights?" he demanded.

"I'm not a cop, Pete," she said, holstering her gun. "I'm a profiler. I'm trying to find this girl's killer. If you didn't do that, you don't have to worry about me testifying about some computer theft. Last chance, twenty seconds. How did you get the laptop?"

"Freeze up there," she heard a voice in the distance yell at them.

Vasquez started to glance back down the alley again.

"Eyes on me," she ordered. "Don't move anything but your lips. Answer my question!"

"Okay. Okay. I saw a dude toss something in an alley dumpster over off Emelita Street in Van Nuys. I was curious. So I checked it out and found the laptop. It didn't even have a hard drive. I just pawned it to make a few quick bucks."

"Describe the dude," she instructed, ignoring the heavy footsteps fast approaching.

"He had on a sweatshirt with a hoodie. But it was dark. I couldn't see anything else."

"What time was this?"

"I don't remember for sure. It was after midnight," he said hurriedly, closing his eyes tightly at the sound of thundering footsteps only feet from him.

A second later, the running stopped. Jessie looked up.

"Identify yourself!" shouted an officer with a buzz cut just five feet from her. His weapon was pointed at her. The other two officers had theirs aimed at Vasquez.

"My name is Jessie Hunt," she said loud and clear. "I'm a criminal profiler based out of Downtown Central Station. My identification is in my front left pants pocket if someone wants to check it. I also have a department-issued sidearm under my jacket on my right hip. I'm going to raise my arms above my head slowly."

"What are you doing here?" Buzzcut demanded.

"I'm investigating a murder in which Mr. Vasquez is a person of interest. I was hoping to have a word with him."

"And did you get that chance?" a familiar voice asked.

Jessie looked behind the officers in front to see Sergeant Costabile's hulking frame emerge from the darkness of the alley. Two other officers stood behind him.

"We were interrupted by your colleagues," Jessie said, careful not to directly answer the question. "But I'd love the chance to have a chat with him under less extreme circumstances."

"I'm afraid you'll have to get in line, Ms. Hunt," Costabile said as he reached down and violently wrenched Vasquez up to a standing position. "Valley Division has a few questions of our own for this monster, er, excuse me, alleged monster."

"I didn't kill anyone!" Vasquez yelled out frantically as Costabile slapped a pair of cuffs on his wrists.

The sergeant gave Jessie a nasty smirk.

"Sounds like the two of you got to chat a little bit after all," he said, as he kicked Vasquez in the back of the leg, sending him to the ground. The suspect's knees rattled as they slammed on the sidewalk and he gasped in pain.

"That's not necessary, Sergeant," Jessie said quietly. "He's not resisting."

"Oh, I definitely felt some imminent resistance," Costabile countered. "He looked like he was about to run. In fact, he just made a move for my weapon."

Before Jessie knew what was happening, Costabile smacked Vasquez in the jaw with the back of his hand, sending the man careening to the ground. Vasquez moaned but didn't try to move.

"Now he's trying to evade arrest," Costabile warned before kicking Vasquez in the gut.

The man lay on the ground, silently writhing in pain. The sergeant looked back up at Jessie sneeringly, daring her to challenge him again. She looked around at the now half dozen officers who'd assembled around them. It occurred to her that standing there, with a weapon in her possession, she wasn't entirely safe herself, even with her hands up.

This wasn't the moment to take Costabile on. He had every advantage. She needed to wait until the odds were more even.

Behind the officers, she saw the youngish man in plainclothes who had rushed into the bar earlier. He was hanging back, trying not to be noticed.

"Detective Strode, I assume?" she called out.

He took a few steps forward into the light and nodded.

"I'm Wiley Strode," he acknowledged, his voice shaky. "You're Hunt, correct?"

"I am," she said, trying to inject him with confidence through the sheer power of her voice. "Since you're in charge here, do you mind if I put my hands down now? We've got our suspect in custody. The scene is relatively secure. Maybe we lower the temperature a bit?"

Strode glanced over uncertainly at Costabile, whose eyes remained fixed on Jessie.

"Do you feel like you have the scene in hand, Sergeant?" Strode asked him deferentially.

Costabile stood silently for a moment, then grabbed Vasquez's hair and yanked his head back hard.

"I'm not sure, Detective. I worry this guy might still be a threat to the safety of our men. He might need a little extra subduing."

Strode swallowed hard but said nothing. Jessie realized he was going to be of no help. As Costabile continued to tug on Vasquez's hair with his left hand, he put his right hand on his nightstick. As he unsnapped its holster, she decided that no matter the odds, she had to act. She was just about to step forward when she heard another voice she knew well.

"Seven on one—you don't think you can handle those odds without your stick, Sergeant Costabile?"

Everyone looked over to see Ryan Hernandez walking jauntily in their direction. One of the officers started to point his gun at him when Costabile warned him off.

"It's okay," he growled reluctantly. "He's a detective from Downtown. No need to shoot him."

"I appreciate that, Sergeant," Ryan said as he came to a stop next to Jessie. "I think the profiler assigned to this case can put her hands down now, don't you?"

He reached up and physically lowered her arms without waiting for an answer. Though his tone was devil-may-care, she could see the concern in his eyes. This situation was still extremely volatile.

"There's some dispute about whose case this is," Costabile retorted. "I believe Detective Strode here might have something to say on the matter."

Strode stepped forward, trying to look cool despite his deer-in-the-headlights vibe.

"I tried to reach you all day, Detective. But you never got back to me. I was hoping to pool resources."

"I'm sorry about that," Ryan said warmly. "I was in court all day and I know Jessie was chasing down leads nonstop. We're happy to do all that now. But maybe we could formally arrest Mr. Vasquez rather than reenacting a scene from *The Purge*. What do you say?"

Strode started to look toward Costabile but Ryan short-circuited that.

"Detective Strode," he said forcefully. "As the Valley Bureau detective assigned to this case in conjunction with HSS, what do *you* say? Shall we take this off the street and handle it professionally? Is that something you'd be on board with?"

Strode, sensing that any future credibility he might have was on the line, nodded.

"That sounds good," he said quietly as he aggressively avoided making eye contact with Costabile, who was staring a hole through him.

"Great," Ryan said, leaping on the nod and running with it. "I think I'll ride with Mr. Vasquez on the way to the station."

"That won't be necessary," Costabile said. "We don't want to burden you with such a mundane task."

"Oh, it's no burden," Ryan said with studied pleasantness. "I'd hate for him to try to hurt himself in some way and put the investigation at risk. In fact, I insist. Sergeant, I'd really appreciate if you could take the lead on heading back to the station right away and securing an interrogation room for Detective Strode and myself. I know you've got some pull. We'll find a squad car for Mr. Vasquez."

Costabile turned his dagger stare to Ryan. He seemed to be weighing whether to fight him on this. Now that the drama of the bar raid had passed, he clearly sensed that he couldn't just throw his weight around without consequence. He opened his mouth but before he could speak, Ryan beat him to it.

"Sergeant," he said, calmly but with finality, "I insist."

CHAPTER EIGHTEEN

Jessie had been shut out.

She sat in the Van Nuys Station bullpen waiting area, trying not to act annoyed that she had been prevented from participating in, or even observing, the interrogation of Pete Vasquez. After about an hour, Ryan emerged, looking troubled.

She stood up as he approached and was about to ask how it went when he shook his head almost imperceptibly. A few moments later Detective Strode followed him into the bullpen. Ryan turned back to the younger detective.

"I'll check in with you first thing tomorrow, Wiley," he said. "In the meantime, it's on you to make sure that Vasquez doesn't have any more unfortunate accidents. You get me?"

Strode hung his head.

"I'll do the best I can," he said unconvincingly.

"Listen," Ryan warned, leaning in close and speaking quietly. "I can't control what goes on in your house. But if anything happens to a guy who you're asserting is a legit murder suspect while he's in your care, it's going to look bad for you. I get that you have to walk around on tiptoes around here. But you also have to look out for yourself. Don't be the fall guy, you understand?"

Strode nodded, though he didn't look like the speech had stiffened his spine that much. Ryan turned and indicated that he and Jessie should leave. As they headed for reception, Costabile walked out of the interrogation area. His eyes immediately fell on Jessie. As she walked out, she could have sworn she saw him blow her a kiss.

Once outside, they walked to Jessie's car. Neither spoke until they were well away from the building.

"So where are we at?" she asked when they finally felt they were away from prying ears.

"Nowhere good," Ryan said resignedly. "Despite my strenuous objections, they're going to charge Vasquez."

"Based on what?"

"Based on his fingerprints on Michaela's laptop and surveillance footage of him pawning it at the shop. He also has no alibi witness for last night at the time of the murder. He claims he was drinking in a park."

"That's it? None of his prints at her apartment? No blood or DNA on his clothes? Nothing turned up where he lives? Just the laptop?"

"Yep," Ryan confirmed. "To be honest, I didn't have much of an argument to make against charging him. We don't have any other suspects right now that are more promising than Vasquez."

"Because no one's looking for them," Jessie pointed out.

"I don't disagree. It's clear that they want to put this thing to bed. No one was interested in hearing about the porn connection or any other possible leads. It was like a train without brakes in there."

"Can you insist on taking over, using HSS authority?"

"I could try," he said skeptically. "But I'm not sure I'd win that battle. The problem is that Vasquez is here now. It's the custodial version of possession being nine-tenths of the law. Prying him loose from this place once they've got him will be a bureaucratic nightmare—one I'm not sure is worth fighting. We might be better off focusing our energy on other leads."

"What other leads?" Jessie asked, frustrated.

"Look, we'll start fresh in the morning. Maybe something will pop by then."

Jessie nodded, trying to move past her dissatisfaction.

"I can give you a ride back to your car," she offered, remembering that he was still parked at the Landing Strip.

"That's okay. I'll rideshare. You should go home and get some sleep. After all, you're not just dealing with a murder case, you're dealing with a teenager too."

"Thanks for reminding me."

Ryan smiled.

"Maybe we could try for another evening together sometime soon?" he suggested. "One that won't be interrupted by an anonymous call about a murder?"

"I'd like that," she said. "Can you guarantee such an evening is possible?"

"In my experience, guaranteeing it jinxes it."

"I didn't know you were superstitious," she teased.

"Neither did I."

Jessie tried not to make a sound.

At just past 1 a.m., she put her stuff down on the kitchen counter and sneaked over to Hannah's room to peek in. The girl seemed to be fast asleep. But just to be safe, she carefully pulled her bedroom door closed. Then she plopped down on the couch, too exhausted to move, much less change out of her clothes.

She knew she should go lie down and get a few hours of rest. But her mind was racing. All kinds of ideas and leads bounced around in her head, none of which she could pursue right now.

Michaela was only seventeen, but with two jobs, she surely had a bank account. Jessie made a note to try to access it tomorrow. She also needed to see if the girl's phone records were ready for review yet. She worried that if Captain Decker bought the Valley Bureau claim that they had their man, he'd refuse to let her follow up on any of this.

She heard a rustling behind her and spun around on the couch to find Hannah coming out of her room.

"What are you doing up?" she whispered unnecessarily.

"I was worried about you," Hannah said with such sincerity that it took her by surprise.

"Oh. Thanks. I'm okay; just frustrated."

"Why?" Hannah asked, sitting down beside her on the couch. "Did the guy get away?"

"Just the opposite, actually. We caught someone. But I don't think he's the killer. Unfortunately, the people holding him disagree. So unless I find a new suspect, the guy may go down for this and there won't be anything I can do about it."

They sat there silently for a while. Eventually Hannah readjusted her legs and Jessie thought she was going to get up. Instead the girl leaned back on the couch and looked up at the ceiling.

"I was thinking about something after you left," she said with less certitude than Jessie was used to.

"What was that?"

"You said Mick came from an abusive background, right?"

"Yeah," Jessie confirmed, noting silently that Hannah had adopted use of the girl's nickname when discussing her. "Her dad was a drinker. It was so bad that she got emancipated at sixteen."

"Okay," Hannah said. "In one of my first sessions with Dr. Lemmon, she suggested I start writing in a journal, so I could get my thoughts down—the ones I wasn't comfortable sharing out loud. But the truth is I was already doing that. I started a few days after our father killed my adoptive parents. I wrote furiously just to get the thoughts out of my head. I probably went through five or six journals before she ever brought it up."

"Uh-huh," Jessie said, nodding. She wasn't certain where Hannah was going with this but didn't want to interrupt.

"I was wondering . . . what if Mick did the same thing?"

"Kept a journal?" Jessie asked.

"Yeah. Think about it. Her mom dies. Her dad is a nightmare. She's living at a Catholic school with nuns watching her every second. Then she leaves and starts doing porn. She seems like the kind of girl who might have some stuff she wanted to get off her chest."

"That makes sense," Jessie said noncommittally.

"I thought so," Hannah said, now leaning in. "If she did keep a journal, I'd be willing to bet there's a lot of material in there that might be useful to someone investigating her death. Assuming you knew where to find it."

Jessie sat with the idea for a moment, letting it sink in. After several seconds, a possibility formed in her head. She turned to Hannah.

"You're a genius," she said.

"What?" Hannah said, blushing.

"I think I know where to go and it can't wait until tomorrow. So for the second time this evening, I'm going to say goodnight and suggest you get some sleep."

She got up and headed over to the counter to collect the things she'd placed there only minutes earlier.

"Where are you going?" Hannah asked.

"I'd tell you," Jessie said. "But then I'd have to kill you."

Hannah frowned but said nothing. Jessie was impressed with her restraint so she threw her a bone.

"But, little sister, if this pans out. I promise I *will* tell you."

She caught a quick hint of a smile on Hannah's face

just as she shut the door.

CHAPTER NINETEEN

The girl waited until she was sure the coast was clear.

Only then did she carefully walk into the room where the laptop rested, its silver branded emblem glinting in the dull overnight moonlight. She made her way over to the dresser and stood there silently for several more seconds. When she was sure the thumping she heard was coming from her own heartbeat, she lifted the screen and turned the laptop on.

The glow from the screen illuminated the entire room and she felt like she had been trapped in a prison yard spotlight. But no one appeared or said a word so she punched in the password that she'd secretly learned and waited for the screen to fill up. It didn't take long.

Her finger hovered over the touchpad for a second longer to make absolutely sure she wouldn't be interrupted. Then she clicked the play button.

After a second of buffering, the movie kicked in. Michaela Penn, aka Melissa Mackenzie, aka Missy Mack, wore a Catholic schoolgirl uniform with an unusually short skirt and had her hair in pigtails. She was skipping down a hallway when she was chastised by a man in what was clearly supposed to be priest attire but looked more like a black turtleneck with a piece of white tape on the collar.

"Young lady, I've warned you about skipping in the halls for the last time," he scolded. "Now get in this room and accept your punishment!"

As Missy shuffled into the room and the "priest" closed the door behind her, Hannah Dorsey switched windows and pulled up Mick's Instagram page. She'd been looking at the girl's social media ever since Jessie left the first time that evening and had only just hopped back into bed before her half-sister unlocked the apartment's front door.

Now she was back at it. As the porn played in the background, she toggled among all of Mick's various feeds, trying to soak up as much as she could about the girl. She somehow felt a deep connection to her.

Hannah had gone through Jessie's file on the girl and learned that she was exactly forty-nine days younger than Mick. Their schools were 6.4 miles apart. Mick's GPA was 3.8 when she graduated. Hannah's was 3.9 when she had to leave school because of her parents' murder. Mick's apartment was 4.7 miles from Hannah's old house.

By checking some of Michaela's photos, she learned that they actually knew at least three of the same people. One of the girls from Hannah's school who had graduated last year had even been in a movie with Mick called *Valley Gals Shall.* It wasn't great.

Of course, those surface connections weren't the true reason Hannah had developed what she would acknowledge was an obsession with the other girl. It ran much deeper than that.

Both of them had been forced to grow up fast. Hannah was painfully aware that most girls she'd gone to school with were fixated on their favorite YouTube influencers and where they could find the best juice bar. She and Mick didn't have that luxury.

Their lives were defined by dead caregivers, abusive or psychotic fathers, and the crushing sense that there wasn't a single person in their lives that they could truly trust. That's the world she and Mick lived in. Or in Mick's case, died in.

Hannah looked at these photos of the dead girl and knew that they were part of an act, an image she projected to the world to protect herself from the damage it wanted to inflict on her. She could see it in the vacant, dead-eyed stare Mick offered the camera in her sex scenes. She saw it in the plastic, forced smile on her face in her social media posts. She saw it in the way Mick's hands always seemed to be curled into tight fists, as if she might have to strike out at a threat at any moment. Hannah recognized all of it. It was like she was looking in a mirror.

By the time Jessie got to Michaela's apartment, it was well past 2 a.m.

She'd considered stopping at Van Nuys Station to get the key but decided the request would draw unwanted attention. Instead, she put on a pair of latex gloves and used a technique she'd learned at the FBI Academy to jimmy the lock. Then she ducked under the police tape and stepped inside.

The apartment was dark and had a faint, rusty smell, which she recognized all too well as the scent remnant of blood. Jessie stood in the hall and took the place in. She tried to imagine Michaela standing beside her, deciding the best place to hide a journal that held her deepest, darkest secrets.

The obvious place to start was her bedroom. She walked to the end of the hall and used her foot to push open the door, which was only slightly ajar. Stepping in, she looked around, trying to think where a seventeen-year-old girl might hide something so precious.

She worked her way around the room, opening dresser drawers, crawling under the bed, and carefully sifting through the contents of the closet. She couldn't explain why, but she had the distinct sense that she wasn't the first person to do this in the last twenty-four hours. Something about the way items rested on counters, desks, and the closet floor suggested that they had been reviewed and replaced, not always in their original location.

After twenty minutes, it became clear that the bedroom was a dead end. She returned to the living room and slowly spun in a small circle, hoping she might notice something she'd missed before. Nothing leapt out at her.

Still, she couldn't shake the feeling that Hannah had been on to something. It just made emotional sense that Michaela would need some sort of safe outlet for her thoughts.

It has to be here somewhere.

She sat down in the middle of the floor and tried to picture Michaela doing the same thing. She pictured the girl here alone in the days before Lizzie moved in. This was her place. She had the run of it before she'd decided to have a roommate. She knew all the secret hiding spots. She knew the places Lizzie wasn't allowed to go.

And that's when an idea occurred to her. Lizzie had said the rent was cheap because she really only used the one bedroom. But the reality was that she generally had free rein. Knowing human nature, if there was some spot that Michaela had told her not to go, that very request would have made such a place tempting.

But there was one part of the apartment Lizzie was unlikely to snoop because there was simply no reason to: her own room.

Jessie got up and went to the bedroom. The door was open. The room was fairly spartan, which reflected both Lizzie's finances and the transient lifestyle of a college student.

She hadn't done much to personalize it, though she did have that cross over her bed, reflecting her acknowledged religiosity. There were two framed watercolors on the wall. In the far corner between the window and the closet was a framed Gustav Klimt print of the iconic *The Kiss*.

Compared to some of the other Klimt works in the rest of the apartment, this one was fairly tame. In the painting, a couple embraced chastely. Still, Jessie found it odd that it was in Lizzie's room. The piece was clearly more Mick's style.

Why would she put it in the other bedroom?

Jessie walked over and looked at the print more closely, her brain tingling slightly. The painting was in this room because that's where Michaela wanted it. She would have hung it before Lizzie moved in. And because Lizzie didn't want to alienate her generous friend, she wouldn't have protested, especially since the image was so unobjectionable. It was actually more romantic than erotic.

Nestled in the corner of the room that didn't belong to Mick and innocuous enough to be overlooked entirely, it was the perfect spot to hide something important. Jessie lifted the frame off the wall, excited to see what was behind it. But there was nothing there besides two nails and painted drywall.

Frustrated, she tried to re-hang the print. But it was heavy and she almost dropped the thing. She put it down and allowed herself a second to regroup before trying again. She lifted it a second time, stunned at how unwieldy it was.

Why is it so heavy?

The tingling in her brain had extended to her extremities. She put the frame down again and stared at it. Then she laid it face down on the ground. Kneeling down, she unfastened the backing and lifted it off.

There, tucked in behind the back of the print, was a large manila envelope, packed full to bursting. Jessie removed and opened it. Inside was cash—more money than Jessie had ever seen in her life. She couldn't begin to guess at the total. There were easily a dozen bundles of bills, all at least an inch thick.

She was tempted to try to count them but knew she was already pressing her luck by being here at all. Lingering to rifle through the envelope was one risk too many.

So she tucked it into the back of her slacks, reassembled the frame, and with much effort, managed to hang it back on the wall. She was just heading for the bedroom door when she heard the sound of the unlocked front door creak open.

Chapter Twenty

J essie pulled out her gun.

As the sound of footsteps got closer, she stood next to the door of Lizzie's room with her back pressed against the wall. Anyone who stepped in would be in point-blank range of her weapon.

She exhaled slowly and as quietly as she could. The footsteps, heavy and clunky, were now right outside the bedroom. They stopped briefly, then continued down the hall. Jessie waited until they had gone several steps past her before poking her head out.

It was too dark to identify the intruder but it was definitely a male. He was trudging loudly toward the back room. Jessie briefly considered sneaking out the front door, confident she wouldn't be noticed.

But what if this was the killer, returning to clean up some evidence that might implicate him or merely to bask in his crime? She couldn't turn her back on that. Before she could stop herself she was moving toward the man with her gun raised. When she was only three feet away, she finally spoke.

"Hey!" she shouted.

The man spun around right into the butt of her gun, which she slammed hard against his forehead. As he fell backward, Jessie flicked on the hall light with one hand while pointing her weapon at him. He hit the ground with a thud, let out a loud moan, and looked up. It was Keith Penn, Michaela's father.

"What the hell are you doing here?" she demanded.

"Owwww," he whimpered.

"What are you doing here, Mr. Penn?" she demanded again. "I better get a good answer in the next five seconds."

He looked up, squinting into the light to see her. After a second, he seemed to recognize who was standing over him.

"I'm Michaela's dad," he said weakly.

"I know who you are. We spoke earlier today in jail. Why aren't you still there?"

He reached up and rubbed his head, as if that would somehow dull the ache.

"They released me when I posted bail," he said. "I'm just here to find something … anything to remember her by. I don't even have a picture."

Jessie lowered her weapon slightly. Penn at least seemed to have sobered up. He wasn't slurring like earlier that day and his eyes were clear.

"Why didn't you ask an officer to bring you by?" she asked with less intensity than before.

"Are you kidding? I just wanted to get out of there. Besides, I didn't think they'd let me enter a crime scene, even if I am her father, at least in name."

"What does that mean?" she asked.

He looked down at the carpet and sighed heavily before answering her.

"It's pretty clear I wasn't much of a dad. Ever since Michaela's mom died, I've been in a downward spiral. That was ten years ago and I just never pulled myself out, even for her."

Jessie could feel her animosity ebbing as her curiosity grew.

"Why not?" she asked.

He looked at her closely, debating whether it was worth trying to explain. He seemed oblivious to the trickle of blood running down his forehead.

"I was always a pretty big drinker," he said quietly. "But once Marnie died, it got out of control. Lots of nights I passed out and Michaela had to put herself to bed. Sometimes she had to make her own dinner, usually dry cereal. I don't even know how she managed to get to school, much less get good enough grades to get into that Catholic school."

"It sounds like she was tough cookie," Jessie offered.

"Yeah. Maybe too tough. After a while, on days when I was half-sober, I noticed that she had become … what's the word, distant?"

"That surprised you?" Jessie asked, stunned that he'd expect anything else.

"No, that's not the right word; more like detached, as if she wouldn't allow herself to have any emotions. She never cried, even if I yelled at her or did worse, which sometimes happened. She seemed to shut off, not just with me, but with everyone. To this day, I still remember a comment from one of her teachers on her report card. She got straight A's but the teacher said she was 'disconnected from the school community and seemed unable to form meaningful bonds.' They sent her to the school counselor but it didn't seem to do much good. I can't help but think I did that to her."

He looked up at Jessie as if seeking absolution. But she had none to offer. He was almost certainly right. It was quite likely that he *had* done this to her. Maybe Michaela had anti-social tendencies already, but having an abusive, alcoholic, absentee father would have greatly exacerbated it.

She got the sense that he didn't know just how far his daughter had gone to achieve any semblance of feeling in her life. He seemed not to know that his dead daughter was a porn actress. And though he probably didn't deserve to be protected from knowing the full extent of the harm he'd caused, Jessie decided not to tell. He was pathetic enough as it was, lying limp and forlorn on the apartment carpet. She didn't need to kick him while he was down.

"You should go, Mr. Penn," she finally said. "You could get in trouble for being here and you don't need any more trouble."

"Okay," he said, getting slowly to his feet. "Why are you here?"

Jessie felt a brief moment of anxiety as she realized it wouldn't do for him to go around talking about her presence here. But it faded quickly.

"I'm investigating Michaela's murder," she said, not mentioning that she was ignoring the niceties of proper police procedure. "I'm looking for evidence to catch her killer."

Penn seemed satisfied with that answer and trudged out toward the front door without further prodding. Jessie followed him, not holstering her weapon but now keeping it at her side. She locked the door from the inside and they stepped outside.

"How did you get here?" she asked.

"My truck is impounded so I took a cab from the motel."

Jessie looked at the time. It was 2:24 a.m. She sighed heavily.

"Tell me where it is and I'll give you a ride," she said.

"You'd do that?" he asked, taken aback.

"I just want to go home and get some sleep," she told him. "That's what I recommend you do too."

He nodded and they made their way to her car. Both were weighed down, he by guilt and grief and she by unresolved questions. Neither spoke again, even when they parted ways.

CHAPTER TWENTY ONE

Hannah had to wake her up.

Through a mix of physical and mental exhaustion, Jessie had slept through both her main and backup alarms. When Hannah shook her gently and noted that it was almost 8 a.m., the time Jessie usually got to work, she nearly pulled a muscle bounding out of bed.

"Whoa," Hannah said. "Slow down there, slugger. I think you've earned the right to go in an hour late. When did you finally crash?"

"I think around three," Jessie said, not certain herself.

Her eyes darted over to the dresser, where she could see the edge of the manila envelope under the jacket she'd sloppily draped across it. Then she quickly returned her attention to her half-sister, who was already dressed and had her backpack slung over her shoulder.

"You were going to tell me where you were going," Hannah reminded her. "That is, assuming you won't have to kill me afterward."

"Yeah," Jessie said, motioning for the girl to follow her into the bathroom, where she grabbed a brush and began dragging it through the bird's nest that was her hair. "I went to Mick's apartment, looking for a journal or something similar. I didn't find one but that doesn't mean it wasn't a good idea. I did find some other potential leads that I missed the first time around. So thanks for the suggestion."

"Sure," Hannah said, trying to hide the slight smile forming at the corners of her mouth.

"Give me ten minutes and I'll be ready to take you to school," Jessie promised before swigging some mouthwash and gargling.

"Don't worry about it," Hannah told her. "I was going to take a Lyft anyway. Not to be rude, but it looks like you could use a few minutes to regroup a little. That'll be easier without me up in your business."

"Are you sure?" Jessie asked after spitting out the mouthwash, wondering who this thoughtful, understanding young woman was but keeping that question to herself.

"No problem. Just keep in touch to let me know how the day shakes out for you."

Jessie stared at her, unable to hide her amazement.

"Do we have some kind of *Freaky Friday* situation going on here? I feel like you've suddenly become the guardian around here."

Hannah offered something close to a genuine smile.

"Don't get too comfortable," she warned as she walked out of the bedroom. "All I'm saying is that a person who goes to bed at three ought to be able to sleep until at least eight. Hopefully you'll return the favor."

"Are you planning to be up until three sometime soon?" Jessie asked.

"Gotta go," Hannah replied chipperly as she headed toward the front door.

Before Jessie could follow up, the door slammed shut.

After a quick shower and text to Ryan saying she'd be in a bit late, Jessie sat down on her bed and studied the manila envelope. She'd wanted to look at it last night but she was so bleary-eyed, she worried that she'd inadvertently miss something important.

She snapped on a pair of gloves and looked inside the envelope again. Then she took out one wad of bills and counted them. There were a hundred of them, most of which were twenties, though there were a few fifties and hundreds sprinkled in. They totaled $3,250.

She dumped out all the other bundles out on the bed and realized she'd vastly underestimated how many there were last night. She'd thought there were a dozen but all told, there were twenty-eight. Assuming all of them were in the $3,000 range, that meant that Michaela had collected in the neighborhood of $85,000.

That was quite a chunk of change to have amassed in less than six months, especially considering that the films she'd done were mostly low budget, bottom of the barrel stuff. More suspicious, despite the sketchy nature of the business Michaela was in, even Lenny Lander wouldn't pay his staff, porn actors or not, in cash. He might want to, but after meeting his mother, Jessie was sure payment was made via check or direct deposit.

In that case, why did Michaela have nearly $100,000 in cash hidden in an envelope behind a painting in her apartment? Even in her shady world, something about the decision felt off. It didn't take a massive deductive leap to guess the reason.

Clearly the girl didn't want to answer questions about where the money came from. And while the bank might not ask, it could still conceivably come to the attention of some other law enforcement or regulatory agency.

Jessie remembered what Hannah had said last night about girls from her school doing private dates in addition to the actual films. The likelihood that Michaela had done the same thing seemed high. Also plausible: the chance that a date had gone badly, ending in her death.

But if all her dating transactions were done in cash, how could her clients possibly be traced? The tech team could eventually get the GPS data for her phone from the wireless company and look at her credit card statements. But that might not prove anything.

If she was seeing these people at her place, when her roommate was off at school, there wouldn't be any credit card records and her location data would be useless. She muddled through the challenge in her head as she started to put the bundles back in the envelope. There was another problem: what to do with all this money.

She couldn't keep it at her place. And she definitely couldn't turn it in to Valley Bureau. If she did that, she was sure it would disappear, whether by graft or simply to prevent it being used as evidence in the case. Even Central Station was a concern, considering the tentacles that Sergeant Costabile and his superiors seemed to have throughout the department.

That left only one realistic option, someone she hadn't spoken to in months and wasn't sure would accept her call. She was about to look up the phone number when she noticed something attached to one of the currency straps. It was a Post-it.

She pulled it off and looked at it. At first she thought a grocery checklist had inadvertently gotten stuck to a wad of bills. But when she peered more closely she discovered that the letters on the note, written in light, hard-to-read pencil, were what appeared to be initials. The first said "D.K." The next was

"M.B." That was followed by "A.R." The last row had two sets: "M.Z. + H.Z." That set had a line through them, as if they had been crossed off.

Jessie stared at the letters, as if looking at them long enough would suddenly unlock some secret code within. But after several minutes, she came to the conclusion that these were almost certainly exactly what they seemed to be, the initials of people Michaela had either "dated" or planned to.

Considering the fact that she had nothing else to go on, she couldn't dismiss this lead entirely. But it felt borderline worthless. Even for the crossed-out dual initials, "M.Z. + H.Z.," the odds of narrowing them down to something useful were minute. Still, it was more than she had five minutes ago. So she copied the initials into her phone, tossed everything back in the envelope, threw on some clothes, and headed out the door to follow any path that might get justice for Michaela Penn.

Chapter Twenty Two

Jessie felt more like a drug dealer than a law enforcement officer.

She waited on a bench in Pershing Square, a few blocks away from Central Station, for her contact to arrive. It didn't take long. Within three minutes of her arrival, he showed up and sat down beside her.

"How's it going, Jessie?" he asked.

"As you know better than most, I've been much worse. How about you, Agent Dolan?"

"Getting by," he said, shrugging.

FBI Agent Jack Dolan seemed to be telling the truth. The last time she'd seen him was several months ago, when they'd worked together on a case that ended in the death of her own serial killer father. By the end of their time together, their mutual animosity had turned into grudging respect.

In the intervening time, Agent Dolan seemed to have turned a corner. She remembered him as a surprisingly paunchy, long-haired, worn-down, hard-drinking cynic who invariably had food stains on his ill-fitting suit.

He still had the bureau-violating long silver hair. But there were no visible stains and he seemed to have lost a considerable amount of weight. He appeared healthy.

"You look good," she told him. "Still surfing?"

"Most mornings," he said conspiratorially. "You can probably smell the salt water on me. I cut out the drinking too."

"Completely?" she asked, stunned as she recalled how he'd downed hard liquor like water.

"I didn't trust myself to do it any other way," he admitted.

"How's it going?" she asked.

"Well, I'm a forty-two-year-old man who drank pretty much every day since I was seventeen, so it's been challenging. But at least I sleep better. What about you? When I got your call, I did a little catch-up on your status. All your serial killer stalkers are dead so you don't have twenty-four-hour protection. You've assumed guardianship of a frickin' teenager. You're dating a detective. It's almost like you're domesticated now."

"How did you know about the dating thing?" Jessie demanded, ignoring her flushing cheeks and all the other stuff he managed to somehow uncover.

"I'm an FBI agent and I'm good at it," he said. "Did you expect any less?"

Jessie smiled despite herself.

"It's just a little disconcerting to hear my personal business thrown back at me so casually. We're trying to keep that last bit quiet, so if you could keep it to yourself?"

Dolan pretended to lock his mouth and throw away the key.

"So why are we here?" he finally asked. "You sounded more anxious than usual on the phone."

Jessie pulled out the envelope and dropped it in his lap. He looked down at it, then back up at her expectantly.

"Long story short," Jessie began, "I'm investigating the murder of an under-age porn actress who may have been an escort on the side. She was stabbed nine times but the folks on the case all seem to want to wrap it up fast and tidy. I'm worried that they have an ulterior motive. So when I found about eighty-five grand in cash hidden in her apartment, I wasn't entirely confident that I could turn it over and expect it be handled properly. So instead, I'm giving it to you until I know what's going on."

"You want the Bureau to take custody of the cash?" he asked.

"No, I want *you* to hold it. I don't know who these cops have under their thumbs but it's clear they have serious reach. If you put this in the system, even at the federal level, I worry it will get back to them. I don't trust the bureaucracy right now. I trust you."

Dolan stared at her for a moment, clearly doing some mental calculations involving risk and reward. Finally he cracked a grin.

"I know just where to keep it safe," he assured her. "You see, there's this yacht I've been looking at . . ."

"I will kill you, Dolan," she growled.

"Just kidding," he said, chuckling. "I have a safe in my office. No one else has the combination. It'll be good there. But I can only hold it for a little while. If this thing is as messy as you suggest, there could be blowback for me too. So I can give you until the end of business tomorrow. After that, it's your hot potato again, okay?"

"That's fair," she said, standing up. "I better get to the office. I'm already almost an hour late and I am, you know, investigating a murder."

"Sure," Dolan said. "Just one more thing before you go. When I was doing my background review on you earlier, the one that told me you're dating Hernandez, something else popped."

Jessie noticed that for the first time since he arrived, Dolan looked uncomfortable.

"Go ahead," she said, apprehensive.

"Your ex-husband, Kyle Voss, is doing his time at the Theo Lacy Facility in Orange County."

"Right," Jessie confirmed. "He was transferred from the Men's Central Jail last year. You're not about to tell me they're releasing him, are you? Because he's got something like sixty-five years left on his sentence, even with good behavior."

"No—nothing like that," Dolan assured her. "In fact, he may have more time added to his sentence. It seems that after a stretch in which he was a model prisoner, he's now fallen in with an unsavory crowd."

"What does that mean?" Jessie asked, her fingers getting prickly and cold.

Dolan looked hesitant to go on but realized that he didn't have a choice at this point.

"He seems to have gotten friendly with a gang associated with one of the cartels. At first, the thought was that it was a desperate move in order to get protection from other potential threats inside. But apparently *he* reached out to them to initiate the relationship."

"How do you know all this?"

"The Bureau has a confidential informant in the gang who periodically passes us info. I wouldn't mention it except that in his last report, he noted that Kyle mentioned you. That's why it was in the file."

"What did he say?" Jessie asked, trying to sound calm.

"Typical stuff you expect from a disgruntled ex-husband who was in prison after being outsmarted by the wife he'd tried to kill."

"Typical stuff like what, Dolan?" she pressed.

"Oh, stuff like that you shouldn't be living it up with money he earned, that you're a fraud who gets credit for crimes you were lucky to solve, that you deserve to be knocked out of your ivory tower, that kind of thing."

"That's all?" Jessie asked skeptically. "Those don't sound like the kind of comments that would make it into an FBI report. And they seem tame for Kyle. After all, the last time I saw him, he told me, what was the exact quote? I think it was that he wanted to take a tire iron and beat me until I was a pulpy mess of shattered bones, shredded skin, and oozing blood."

"Yeah," Dolan said, reluctantly going on. "It sounds like he hasn't exactly mellowed since then. He might have also mentioned to his new friends that he'd like to gut you like a pig and bathe in your warm blood."

Neither spoke for a moment. Jessie gulped hard before responding.

"Okay. Well, that's not ideal."

"No," Dolan agreed. "But let's keep it in context. He's in prison. You put him there. He's a murderer trying to get in tight with some scary guys. It's not a stunner that he'd say something like that."

Jessie nodded. That was all true.

"Any evidence that he's done anything other than *talk* about fantasies of my death?" she asked.

"None," Dolan said definitively. "And as soon as I saw the report, I passed the word to our C.I.'s handler for him to alert us the second that changes. I almost didn't mention it. But I figured you deserved to know. Besides, if anyone can handle something like that, it's you."

She wasn't sure she could but she didn't want Dolan to feel bad about telling her so she forced a smile to her lips.

"You did the right thing," she assured him. "Frankly, that's about fifth on my list of concerns these days."

She said it with such confidence that she thought he almost believed her.

CHAPTER TWENTY THREE

"I think we're about to get shut down."

Those were Ryan's first words to Jessie the second she walked into the bullpen ten minutes later.

"Why do you say that?" she asked, forgoing any pleasantries of her own.

"Valley Bureau has officially charged Vasquez," he said. "They're pushing hard to close the case. I told Captain Decker that we're not on board with that. He wants to meet with us at nine thirty to make our pitch for keeping it open. Other than Valley's sloppy, stunningly suspicious rush to judgment, I don't have anything hard to offer. Without something definitive, I think he's going to defer to them."

"In that case," she said, pulling out her phone and scrolling to her note with the initials from the Post-it, "it's a good thing I found these."

"What's that?" he asked, squinting at the letters.

"For your own professional deniability, I can't tell you where I got it," she warned. "But this is a list of initials that I think represent people Michaela had private dates with."

"She did that?"

"I can't prove it. But there is good reason to think she did and this list was an informal way to track her clients. I'm hoping we can use it to come up with some names."

Ryan looked at her doubtfully.

"We can go through her data," he said, patting the file on her desk. "But the chances of narrowing down something credible based solely on a bunch of initials from a source you won't even share with me are ... not great."

"Which is why we need to get started," Jessie countered. "We've got less than a half hour until nine thirty. Let's make the most of it."

Jessie quickly went through most of Michaela's banking and credit card records and was planning to look at her phone logs next. Across from her, Ryan reviewed the GPS data from her phone. She had come across a few names that matched initials but so far, they'd all turned out to be dead ends.

"Hernandez and Hunt—in my office!" Decker shouted across the bullpen, making Jessie jump out of her seat.

She looked up at the wall clock and saw that thirty minutes had passed in the blink of an eye. As she followed Ryan to Decker's office, she mentally scrambled, trying to come up with any credible reason for the captain to let them stay on the case. There were several she found compelling but she doubted he'd agree.

"Close the door," he ordered as she entered.

She did so, and then took a seat beside Ryan.

"So I gave you the day, Hunt," Decker said, settling into his worn swivel chair. "And it looks like you didn't catch any murderers in that time. Am I mistaken?"

"Not yet, sir," she conceded.

"Well, our friends in Valley Bureau believe they have."

"They're wrong, sir," Jessie said forcefully. "I was the one who apprehended Pete Vasquez. I questioned him before anyone else arrived on the scene. He's not our man."

"Are you sure about that, Hunt?" he asked pointedly.

"That is my belief, sir."

"Well, those aren't exactly the same thing, are they? Unfortunately, the folks at Valley Bureau are confident enough in Vasquez's guilt that they're formally charged him with Michaela Penn's death. He's being arraigned this afternoon. Unless you have another suspect for me, I'm not sure what can be done."

"Captain," Jessie pleaded, "Vasquez is a small-time thief. He has no history of violence and his claim about finding the laptop in an alley dumpster is as credible as any assertion that he got it at her apartment. I looked at the CSU report this morning. None of his DNA or fingerprints was found at her place. Everything about his arrest looks like a cover-up."

That hung in the air for a second.

"What do you mean, Hunt?" Decker asked, leaning forward.

"Nothing, Captain," Ryan said quickly. "Jessie's just spitballing."

"Is that true, Hunt? Because that's quite an allegation you just made."

Jessie glanced at Ryan, who appeared to be trying to will her to stay quiet with the power of his stare. Though she didn't want to rein herself in, the intensity of his gaze gave her pause.

"Captain," she said slowly, "I don't like how this investigation has been run. It's been sloppy and unprofessional at best and...more than that at worst. But am I formally alleging something untoward on the part of members of Valley Bureau? Not at this time, sir."

"All right," Decker said, leaning back in his chair again. "That was just about the most hedged non-accusation I've ever heard. And I'm going to choose to remember it as full-throated support for your colleagues in the LAPD. That's what my notes will reflect for the record."

"Yes, sir," she said reluctantly.

"I'm deferring to the wishes of the team in Valley Bureau and officially pulling HSS from the case. That frees you both up to handle this. A country club tennis coach in Hancock Park was found dead on the court this morning. It looks like he was bludgeoned with a racket. The head of security is expecting you within the hour."

He tossed a thin file across his desk at them.

"Yes sir," Ryan said, grabbing the file as he stood up.

Jessie stood up too and followed him to the door without a word. She was almost out when Decker called her back.

"Hunt," he said firmly. "Just so we're clear on this. Valley Bureau is handling the Penn case. You are not. Got it?"

"Yes sir," she said with the level of enthusiasm she felt.

Ryan was waiting for her outside the office. Despite her strong desire, Jessie refrained from yelling at him right then and there.

"Way to have my back," she hissed in a loud whisper.

"I *did* have your back," he insisted. "You were this close to Decker calling in Internal Affairs to start a full-on investigation."

"Would that be so bad?" Jessie challenged. "This seems like exactly the kind of thing that I.A. should be looking into. Chatty Cathy obviously thought so too."

"No, Jessie. She didn't. That's why she called me. Chatty Cathy's calls have consistently been about trying to solve cases, not catching dirty cops. For all we know, she could have inside knowledge about these cases because she's dirty."

Jessie couldn't believe what Ryan was saying.

"So you don't want these guys—whoever's directing Costabile—brought to justice?" Jessie demanded.

"Of course I do," Ryan retorted. "But that wasn't my priority and it wasn't Chatty Cathy's either. Solving the case was. There was a finite window to solve this one before it got swallowed up and now the window has closed. It's happened with other cases she tipped me off to and it's happened here. I'm not happy about it but it's out of my hands now."

Jessie started to protest but Ryan cut her off.

"Decker was very clear," he reminded her. "Pursuing this after he formally took us off it would have serious repercussions. Plus, we have no idea who's involved. I'm concerned about what these people are capable of if we keep pushing."

They stared at each other, both furious, neither speaking. Ryan finally relented.

"I have to go to the bathroom. When I get back, I'm hoping we can put this behind us and go investigate this ridiculous case about the tennis coach beaten to death with a racket. I'll see you in five minutes."

Jessie watched him go, fighting the urge to cuss him out in front of everyone. When he disappeared from sight, she took several deep breaths and turned back to the bullpen. As she did, she swore she saw about a dozen sets of colleagues' eyes suddenly dart elsewhere.

Pretending not to notice, she returned to her desk, sat back down, and caught sight of the phone logs she was no longer supposed to review. Despite what Decker said, she couldn't help but glance over the names for any initials that matched the Post-it list. There were none. But she did notice something else.

The same name appeared on both a canceled check from the bank and a cell phone call: Helen Vance. The initials didn't match any from the Post-it. But it was the first time she'd come across the same person on two separate lists. She punched the name into the LAPD database. When her computer screen showed the result, she had to force herself not to gasp.

Helen Vance didn't have a record. But apparently she did have another name. In addition to Vance, she apparently also went by her full married name, Helen Vance-Zellers and even sometimes just by Helen Zellers—H.Z. Helen was married to a man named Matthew Zellers—M.Z.

M.Z. + H.Z. The crossed-out initials.

Jessie looked up to make sure no one had noticed the jolt of electricity that had just shot through her entire body. Everyone seemed oblivious. She scribbled down the contact info for the couple and then closed the browser tab.

Ryan was walking back from the restroom with a look of grim determination on his face. She knew what that meant. He was preparing himself for the unpleasant task of convincing her that they needed to move on and not rock the boat. She decided to save him the effort.

"I have to go," she said, standing up to meet him. "Can you get started on the tennis coach case without me?"

"You have to go? That's all the information you're giving me?" he asked incredulously.

"I have to take care of something. If it comes up, you can tell people that I said it was about Hannah."

"Is that true?" he asked.

Jessie stared at him, not sure how best to answer that.

"It's the reason I'm giving you," she finally said. "That's the best I can do."

She grabbed her bag and headed out of the bullpen, refusing to look back at what she was certain was Ryan's disapproving face.

Chapter Twenty Four

Jessie rode the wave of anger.

She knew that once it faded, the consequences of what she was doing now—going to see the Zellers—would hit her. And if she started thinking about the fact that she was following up a lead on a case she was expressly prohibited from pursuing, she might lose her courage.

So she channeled the anger as long as she could. As she made her way to the Zellers's Beverly Hills mansion, she tried not to let doubt creep into her head. Everything in her gut told her this was more than just a robbery gone wrong.

The call from Chatty Cathy seemed to reinforce that. But despite all the suspicious behavior on the part of the guys from Van Nuys Station—mishandling the crime scene and body, homing in on only one suspect, and so much more—the truth was, she didn't have anything definitive to say they were wrong.

Yes, the crime felt more personal than a robbery. And Michaela's lifestyle and work—both on and off the books—suggested she interacted with some unsavory types. But none of that was proof of anything. Pete Vasquez had the laptop stolen from her apartment. Based on that alone, she had to acknowledge that he was a legitimate suspect.

Was it possible she was overcomplicating things? Was she making it personal because Michaela reminded her so much of Hannah? If the victim was a twenty-six-year-old Latina from East L.A. instead of a teenage girl from the Valley, would she still be pushing like this? The question made her squirm uncomfortably in the driver's seat.

Luckily, she didn't have to think about it any longer. The Zellers's home was up ahead. She forced all other thoughts from her head and focused on the people she was about to meet. They lived on Benedict Canyon Drive, north of the Beverly Hills Hotel, just before the street began to climb and turn into a steep, winding hill road.

The house was set back off the street, with a long driveway. As she pulled in, Jessie reminded herself of the couple's background. Matthew Zellers was a producer on the long-running TV crime procedural *Catch & Convict*. Helen was a party planner. They'd been married for seven years, were in their late thirties, and had no children. Matthew had never been arrested. Helen's sole run-in with the law was at a college protest nearly two decades ago.

Jessie pulled up to the house and walked to the front door, taking in the massive plantation-style entrance, complete with enormous white pillars. She rang the bell and waited, fully expecting it to take a while for someone to get all the way to the front.

But within ten seconds the door opened to reveal an attractive, petite woman with blonde ringlets wearing tights and a sports bra. She looked like she'd been in the middle of a workout.

"Can I help you?" she asked, slightly out of breath. There were droplets of sweat on her forehead.

"I hope so. I'm Jessie Hunt with the LAPD. I'm looking for Matthew and Helen Zellers."

"Well, you found half of them," the woman said. "I'm Helen. Did you say you were with the police?"

"Yes. I'm a profiler for the department. I was hoping I could ask a few questions."

"Sure. Come on in," she said, waving Jessie inside. "I was just finishing my leg day. Do you consult for the show? Matt didn't say anyone would be coming by today."

"No, Mrs. Zellers. This is unrelated to your husband's work. I was actually hoping to speak to both of you."

Helen was walking quickly ahead of her down the hall, which opened into a large kitchen. She seemed unfazed by a random person showing up requesting to question her. Jessie wondered how often it happened.

"Matt's upstairs working. I'll call him down," she said, opening the fridge and pulling out a pitcher of thick green liquid. "Did you want some celery juice while we wait?"

"No, I'm good," Jessie assured her.

Helen nodded as she grabbed her phone.

"Hey, sweets," she said when a male voice answered. "There's an LAPD profiler down here who wants to talk to us. Can you come down for a sec?"

The voice said something Jessie couldn't pick up.

"I don't know," Helen replied before turning to Jessie. "What's this about?"

"I'd rather explain it to both of you together."

"She'll tell us when you come down," Helen said into the phone. "Just hurry up. The anticipation is killing me."

The voice responded and there was a click.

"He'll be right down," Helen said, motioning to one of the barstools at the kitchen island. "Why don't you have a seat?"

"Thank you," Jessie said, selecting one.

"This is all very exciting," Helen said enthusiastically. "The biggest item on my list for the day was to get my nails done. And now I have a real-life profiler in my house. What did you say your name was again—Clarice? I'm just kidding."

She giggled to herself before taking a long glug of the celery juice. Jessie felt mildly ill watching her. A few seconds later, Matthew Zellers walked through the door.

He was not what Jessie imagined a television writer for a crime show would look like. Easily six foot two and 210 pounds, he looked more like a body-builder than a guy who spent hours behind a computer screen. She wondered if he wished he was in front of the camera rather than behind it. He smiled broadly at Jessie.

"Have you come to criticize the show's vérité elements?" he asked as he stood next to his wife. "Because I'll tell you what I tell the other law enforce-ment types who like to complain. I work on a television show. It's not real life."

Somehow he managed to sound friendly despite the charged comment. Jessie noted that the couple's proximity to each other would make studying their reactions to her questions much easier.

"I'm not interested in your show," she said sharply, deciding it was time to take charge of the conversation. "I need to talk to you about something else entirely. Do you know a woman named Michaela Penn?"

The Zellers wore matching clueless expressions.

"I don't think so," Matthew said. "The name doesn't ring a bell."

"What about Melissa Mackenzie?"

That question got a different reaction. The look the couple exchanged this time was much more knowing.

"We know Melissa well," Helen said. "Why?"

"She's dead," Jessie said flatly.

She added nothing more, watching to see how they'd respond. Both of their faces fell at the same time. They looked genuinely stunned and in Helen's case, devastated.

"Are you sure?" Matthew asked.

"I am," Jessie said, pressing ahead, intentionally not letting them get their bearings. "Her real name was Michaela Penn and she was murdered the night before last. What can you tell me about your relationship to her?"

Again the couple looked at each other. This time, there was uncertainty on both their faces.

"I wouldn't say we had..." Matthew began.

"Before you answer, Mr. Zellers," Jessie interrupted, "please remember that if I'm talking to you, I obviously have a general sense of the circumstances. So please don't insult me by trying to dissemble. You can save us all some time by just being forthright."

Neither Zellers spoke for several seconds. Helen finally cleared her throat.

"We were close," she said quietly. "I assume you know about what she did for a living?"

"How close?" Jessie asked, ignoring the question directed at her.

Matthew took over.

"I saw one of her videos and reached out to her. Helen and I have a very...accommodating relationship and she agreed that Melissa, should she be interested, might add a little spice to our home life."

"You can dispense with the euphemisms, Mr. Zellers," Jessie said.

His brow furrowed.

"I want to be direct, Ms. Hunt," he said. "We want to help in whatever way we can. But as you might gather, we have some apprehension about how what we say might be used against us. Can you give us assurances that that you're only looking for information about Melissa's death and not other legal indiscretions?"

"I can't make any promises other than to tell you finding Michaela's killer is my top priority," Jessie said. "Other violations of law are secondary at this point."

She wanted to give them the room to be honest but wasn't going to foreclose on the possibility of pursuing people who were paying for sex with an underage girl.

"Matthew," Helen said, her voice quavering, "let's tell her what we know. We can handle any consequences for our actions. If anything we tell Ms. Hunt can help find out who did this, we should speak up."

Matthew weighed her words briefly before nodding.

"I contacted her through an agency called Courtesan Companions. They connect porn actresses with people who want to be with them in person," he said. "She reached out and we set something up."

"What exactly does that mean—set something up?" Jessie asked.

Matthew sighed deeply before reluctantly continuing.

"Well, there's an elaborate screening process. First, I put down a deposit—a thousand dollars—to cover all the costs and pay for her time if I backed out for some reason. Then the agency did identity verification and a background check. Once those were complete, I got tested for STDs and provided the results. She did the same."

"What about you, Mrs. Zellers?" Jessie wanted to know.

Helen looked taken aback.

"Oh, I didn't participate. That was just between them."

"I see," Jessie said, trying to hide her surprise. "So what happened next?"

"She came over and we talked for a while. Once she felt comfortable, we got down to the business she was there for."

"Can you be more specific?"

Matthew blushed for the first time since he'd come downstairs.

"I'd rather not," he said. "Let's just say that she was willing to role play some of my fantasies. If you know the general scenarios in her films, you can probably draw accurate conclusions about what we did."

Jessie looked over at Helen, who seemed less uncomfortable than she would have guessed.

"And there was no jealousy?" Jessie asked her.

Helen shrugged.

"We were honest with each other before we got married," she said. "Matt was upfront about certain things he was into that I wasn't, so we came to this accommodation. It works for us. Besides, Meliss . . . er, Michaela and I did other things together."

"What kind of things?"

"Nothing like what you're thinking, Ms. Hunt," Helen said firmly.

"Clear it up then."

"It's going to sound weird."

"Believe me," Jessie said. "I'm up to date on weird."

"Okay," Helen said with a shrug. "We kind of became friends. We'd go shopping together. I'd buy her outfits. We even baked a few times, right in this kitchen."

"You did these things with the person playing fantasy sex games with your husband?" Jessie confirmed.

Helen didn't respond at first. She looked like she was struggling to come up with the right words.

"Look, Melissa—I'm just going to call her that since that's how I knew her—Melissa's mom died when she was young and she told me her dad wasn't really around. I can't have kids. I know it sounds crazy but we developed kind of a bond, maybe not mother-daughter, but something close to it. We liked hanging out. I never thought about that other stuff when it was just the two of us."

As unusual as the situation sounded, Jessie didn't find it unbelievable. As someone who lost her own mother young, she knew the power of any maternal figure willing to offer emotional support and companionship. It was the reason she felt so drawn to Dr. Lemmon.

"Can you explain something else to me?" she said. "I found both your initials on a piece of paper at her apartment but they were crossed off. Why would that be?"

Matthew looked away but Helen stared straight at Jessie.

"I don't know for sure but I think I can guess," she said softly before pausing.

"You've come this far, Mrs. Zellers," Jessie pressed. "You may as well go all the way."

Helen nodded, sighed deeply, and continued.

"We'd had this arrangement for a couple of months. But about a week ago, Melissa came to me and said she didn't feel comfortable doing . . . what she'd been doing with Matt anymore in light of the time we'd been spending together. She said it felt too strange."

"How did you react to that?" Jessie asked.

"I understood," Helen replied. "But the very reason we got involved with her in the first place was for him. So it became this untenable situation. She didn't want to be with Matt anymore. But she and I couldn't realistically go on trips to the mall and leave him hanging. So we all agreed it had to end."

"And everybody was cool with that?"

"I wouldn't say 'cool,'" Matthew admitted. "But we were all adults so we made the best of it."

"Are you sure you weren't a little more upset than that, Mr. Zellers?" Jessie tweaked. You're a powerful, wealthy TV producer and you're getting the brush-off from this underage nobody?"

"Wait, what?" he said, his voice rising.

"Yeah, that's the other thing," Jessie said. "Michaela wasn't an adult like the two of you. She was seventeen. You were technically paying for sex with a child."

Chapter Twenty Five

"No, no, no," Matthew said, as if repeating it over and over would make it untrue. "That can't be."

"It is. And I don't need to tell you, the sentence for something like that can be significant."

Jessie actually had no idea what the sentence was. And she didn't really want to get too deep in the weeds anyway. Without the LAPD to back her up, she was in a vulnerable position. If the Zellers called a lawyer, Jessie's lack of authorization for this interview would be quickly revealed. She needed to scare them, but not too much.

"I had no idea she was underage," Matthew balked. "And you said any legally questionable activities weren't a priority for you."

"I did," she agreed. "And that still stands. What you did isn't excusable. But assuming you cooperate completely right now, it might be manageable."

"What do you need?" Helen asked.

"First, where were you both on Monday night?"

Matt scrunched up his face trying to remember. But Helen had no such issues.

"We were at the premiere, remember?" she said to him.

"Oh yeah," he recalled, turning to Jessie. "One of the actors on *Catch & Convict* is starring in an action movie being released on Friday. We went to the premiere screening. There was a red carpet beforehand and an after-party. I'd say we have about a hundred and fifty alibi witnesses."

Jessie was annoyed at how happy he seemed at the possibility that he was definitely off the hook. But she tried to stay focused on the crucial issue.

"Okay. We'll check into that. I also need the names of any other clients she had."

Both of their faces fell.

"We don't know that," Helen said. "Melissa was scrupulous about keeping the identities of her clients confidential."

"Even with you?" Jessie challenged. "No gossip over cookie baking?"

Helen shook her head.

"No way," she insisted. "I think she knew that it would ruin her business. If she was willing to tell me about someone else, she knew I'd worry she was telling someone else about us."

"You're sure?" Jessie pushed. "I can claim I got the name from an anonymous source."

"No, she never mentioned a name," Helen reiterated.

Jessie sat silently in her chair. She thought she'd had this great lead that would break open the case. But now it was turning into just another dead end. And she'd pursued it at great risk to her career. If the Zellers ever mentioned this meeting to anyone, she'd be screwed.

She was briefly tempted to warn them not to discuss this with anyone else as a means of protecting herself. But the idea made her feel dirty and she dismissed it. Suddenly Helen's head popped up. Jessie could see she'd had an epiphany of some kind.

"What?" she asked.

"Melissa never *said* anything to me. But she did give me something. About a week and a half ago, just a few days before she brought up her uneasiness with our arrangement, she gave me an envelope. She asked me to keep it for her, said that she'd pick it up at some point. She didn't say what was in it, but I could tell it was important to her. I kept it in the living room between some magazines. I showed her where in case she needed it and I wasn't here."

She left the room and came back a minute later with a sealed envelope. She handed it to Jessie.

"Maybe it'll help?" she said hopefully.

"Maybe," Jessie agreed, not willing to open it front of them. "I'm going to see myself out. But this isn't necessarily over. I'm looking for a killer. But that doesn't mean you're off the hook. Keep your noses clean."

Both Zellers nodded vigorously as Jessie left the kitchen. She made sure to walk down the hall to the front door at a normal, unhurried pace. She didn't rip open the envelope until she was back in her car.

They were photos.

Inside the envelope were photos of three men, all taken while they slept. Jessie didn't recognize any of them. She was debating how to best identify them when her phone rang. It was Captain Decker. Her heart sank.

"This is Hunt," she said, trying to sound upbeat. "What's up, Captain?"

"Where are you right now?" he demanded.

"I'm looking into a personal issue," she said carefully.

"That's interesting. Because I thought I ordered you and Hernandez to handle that tennis coach murder."

"Yes, Captain," she said as soothingly as she could. "I just resolved the issue and was about to join him."

"Hunt, let me be clear. If I find out that you are pursuing the Penn murder, after I explicitly pulled you off it, you will be brought up on disciplinary charges. Do I make myself clear?"

"Yes sir."

Decker hung up without another word.

When Jessie pulled up to the Beverly Country Club in Hancock Park, Ryan was just walking out of the clubhouse.

"Solve the case yet?" she asked cheekily as she got out of her car.

"Pretty much," he answered.

"You're serious?" Jessie said, impressed.

"Yup," Ryan answered, unable to hide a proud smile. "The tennis coach, Paulo Risotre, was actually killed in the men's locker room. His head was smashed in with a glass vase. Then he was dragged out to the court and the killer smashed him a few more times with a racket, which was left near the body. We have footage of the killer moving the body outside. He was wearing a hoodie but we think we know who he is."

"How's that?" Jessie asked.

"Because afterward, this genius in the hoodie got into a car and drove off. Surveillance footage caught the license plate. It belongs to a club member named

Warren Cresper. Talk around the club is that Paulo was giving more than just tennis lessons to Cresper's wife, Maddy. Now we're just waiting for fingerprints on the vase and racket to come back."

"What does Cresper say?" Jessie wanted to know.

"Conveniently enough, Mr. Cresper is currently booked on a three-fifteen flight to Bahia Blanca, Argentina. We have people headed to LAX now to greet him before he leaves."

"Wow," Jessie marveled. "It sounds like you've got this thing all squared away without my help."

"Yeah, well, we're not dealing with a criminal mastermind here. But I'm not sure Decker's going to consider that an excuse for you to go off pursuing 'personal' issues."

Jessie decided to let the mild dig slide.

"He already expressed his displeasure," she conceded. "If it turns out my business wasn't legitimately personal, he's submitting me for disciplinary action."

Ryan shook his head.

"Then I sure hope it was worth it."

"It wasn't personal, Ryan," she said flat out. "I'm sure you're shocked to hear that. But I do think it was worth it. I was following up a lead and I think it's promising."

"Why are you telling me this?" he asked.

"Because I need to know if you think this is legit or if I'm just chasing my tail here. I'm starting to lose perspective."

He shook his head.

"You realize that by asking for my thoughts, you're technically involving me in the case and putting me at risk of discipline?"

"Ryan," she said reassuringly, "we're just two co-workers having a friendly chat in the parking lot. I don't think your pension is at risk here."

"I'm glad you're so confident," he said testily.

"Should I not ask?" she retorted, feeling a little snippy herself.

He sighed. She knew she was pushing the bounds of what was appropriate in both their professional and personal relationships. But there was no one whose opinion she trusted on this more than his. It occurred to her that it couldn't hurt to say that.

"Listen," she continued. "I'm sorry for putting you in this position. If you want, we can forget I brought it up. It's just that I'm in the weeds here and what you think matters to me. I value your perspective. But I can investigate it without you if you prefer. Just know that either way, I'm not giving up on this case, regardless of the consequences."

Ryan's expression was hard to read. His lips were pursed into a grimace but his eyes suggested something else.

Admiration maybe?

"What's your lead?" he finally asked.

She smiled and leaned over to give him a peck on the cheek.

"I figured out who some of those initials belonged to," she said. "H.Z. plus M.Z. They turned out to be a married couple in Beverly Hills. The guy was paying to sleep with Michaela. They both appear to have an alibi for that night but for reasons I can explain later, they were holding on to an envelope she gave them. It had photos of what I believe are other clients of hers. The problem is that I don't recognize any of them and I'm worried that putting them through the system will alert the wrong people that I'm still poking around. I was hoping you might have some suggestions."

"Let me think about it," he said, his brow crinkling in concentration. "Can I see the photos?"

Jessie handed the envelope over and Ryan thumbed through the contents. When he got to photo of the third man, he froze.

"What is it?" she asked.

"I know this guy," he said. "He's a cop."

Chapter Twenty Six

Jessie didn't know whether to be excited or scared. Ryan's expression suggested it should probably be the latter.

"That's not a stunner, is it?" she asked. "Considering all the strange behavior from Costabile and the other guys at Van Nuys Station, the probability that she had a cop as a client was pretty high. I'm just surprised it's not Costabile himself."

"You don't get it, Jessie," Ryan replied, not noticing that he'd lowered his voice even though there was no one around. "This isn't just any cop. And he's not from Van Nuys Station, or even Valley Bureau in general. This is Commander Mike Butters."

"Mike Butters?" she repeated. "One of the initials was M.B."

"I really wish it wasn't," Ryan replied. "Butters heads the Force Investigation Group. He's like, the sixth highest ranking member of the entire LAPD. This is bad."

"How bad?" Jessie asked, already feeling like ice water had started coursing through her veins.

He looked at her with more apprehension than she'd ever seen when he was taking on a criminal.

"Really bad," he said gravely. "It explains everything. Butters used to run Valley Bureau before he got bumped up. Costabile was one of his guys. Everyone in that bureau has some kind of connection to him. It explains why the investigation would be given to a junior detective who could be pushed around, why the body might be inadvertently cremated, why the father was snatched up right in the time window when he could have prevented that."

Jessie gulped hard.

"Are you saying a whole bureau covered up a murder by a senior commander?" Jessie asked, disbelieving.

"No. This doesn't prove Butters had anything to do with Michaela's death. We should definitely check into who the other guys in those photos are. But if he found out about her murder early on, he'd have reason to shut down the investigation quickly anyway. He had to know that a full inquiry would uncover his connection to her. Even if he didn't know she was underage, we're talking about a senior LAPD commander paying an adult film actress for sex. That's not just a career-ender. It's cause for prosecution. He must have just hoped that shutting it down would prevent future questions."

Jessie nodded. All of that made sense. Even the best-case scenario was troubling. Of course, there were far worse scenarios.

"So we're in the crosshairs of a guy who could destroy both of us, even if he's not a killer," she noted. "But what if he is?"

"What do you mean?" Ryan asked.

"What if he did kill her? She was stabbed nine times. If he was willing to do that to keep his secret, who knows what he'd be willing to do to us?"

"You're right," Ryan said. "It's probably a good thing we got put on this tennis coach case. I'm sure Butters is having us watched. If he sees that we're going about our regular business, he might pull back on that."

"You think he's having us tailed?"

"I'd bet money on it," he replied. "Is there any way he could trace this couple you talked to earlier to Michaela?"

Jessie thought about it for a second.

"I don't think so," she finally said. "It's not obvious that they're connected. I only found them because of the initials, which were on a Post-it hidden in her apartment. I seriously doubt anyone had access to it. Do you think he'd have his people question them?"

"Only as a last resort," Ryan said. "He'll know we're assigned to this tennis coach case. If he can't see a connection between this Beverly Hills couple and Michaela, he might assume your visit was related to Paulo Ristore's death. He likely won't want to risk having his people approach them if he can avoid it. You might consider mentioning their interview in our case report to keep him off the scent. It's unorthodox, but necessary, I think."

If she hadn't already known it, Jessie would have been convinced of the seriousness of the situation by Ryan's willingness to have her fudge an interview report. He was a straight shooter and suggesting such a move was out of character for him.

"Here's the other thing," she said, almost afraid to bring up the concern that that been weighing on her. "Decker pulled us off the Penn case. He assigned us to this one. Do you think he's in on it?"

Ryan was quiet for several seconds before responding.

"Never say never," he finally said, "but I don't think so. It's true that he pulled us off the case. But he also pulled strings to get HSS on it in the first place. Why would he do that if he was part of this? And he only pulled us when we didn't have any firm evidence for him. As to this new case, I don't know. He could have just assigned it to us to keep us from being tempted to pursue the Penn case. Or maybe he senses something is off and wants to keep us away from this to protect us. Is it possible that he's dirty? Anything's possible. But I've known the man for close to a decade and I've never had cause to doubt him before. All the same, maybe we find another way to ID the other two guys in those photos Michaela took."

Jessie immediately thought of a potential resource and briefly debated whether to share it with Ryan. But she decided that at this point, he was already in too deep to be protected from repercussions. She might as well tell him everything.

"We can give the photos to Jack Dolan. Your remember him—the FBI agent from that Studio City stabbing case a few months ago?"

"Of course I remember him. You think he'd help?"

"Yeah, I'm pretty sure," she replied slowly.

"Why do you say that like you're the cat who ate the canary?"

Jessie smiled sheepishly.

"Because I may have already reached out to him on something else."

"Care to share?" Ryan asked.

Jessie told him about her late-night visit to Michaela's apartment, the discovery of the envelope, and her handoff of the cash to Dolan.

"I'm sorry I didn't tell you before but I was trying to keep your hands clean."

"I understand," he replied. "But they're completely muddy now so please don't hold out on me anymore."

"I won't."

She sent Dolan screenshots of the men and then turned back to Ryan.

"Now what?" she asked.

"Let's go back to the station," he suggested. "There's nothing more we can do about Michaela for now. But we can continue to look busy on the Paulo Ristore case. Maybe CSU has fingerprints for us."

Jessie agreed. She said goodbye and was just returning to her car when her phone rang. She didn't recognize the number but decided to answer anyway.

"Hello?" she said.

After an unusually long silence, a digitally altered voice responded.

"Stop now. Hannah has been through enough already. Do you want her to suffer more?"

Then the line went dead.

"Ryan!" she screamed.

He was halfway to his car but sprinted back over immediately.

"What is it?" he asked breathlessly.

She told him what the caller had said.

"We have to go check on her," she insisted.

"Of course," he said. "Where would she be right now?"

Jessie looked at the time: 11:37.

"She'd still be at the school she started at last week."

"Okay. Give me the address and I'll follow you there. You call her directly while I call for a unit to get over there now. They'll do a welfare check and stay until we arrive."

She gave him the address, hopped in the car, and immediately called Hannah. It went straight to voicemail.

Stay calm. The school makes them turn off their phones during class. That's all this is.

But knowing it was normal not to be able to reach her and believing it were two different things. As she zigzagged through midday traffic on the longest twelve-minute drive of her life, Jessie called the front office. She got voicemail for that too.

"This is the administrative office. We're sorry no one is able to take your call. Please listen to the list of options and select your preference. A staffer will respond at the earliest possible convenience."

Jessie screamed at the automated message as she punched in "0." The action had no impact. She wanted to throw the phone but instead forced herself to listen to the phone tree choices, trying to determine who was most likely to actually be at their desk. When she heard that she should dial "6" for the library, she decided that was as good a choice as any.

Someone picked up on the third ring.

"Library," the whispered female voice said. "Please hold."

"No!" Jessie yelled. "This is an emergency."

"I'm sorry," the voice said, clearly startled.

"My name is Jessie Hunt. I work for the Los Angeles Police Department. My sister is a student there. A threat was just made against her. Her name is Hannah Dorsey. I need you to go to the head of campus security, have them determine her current location, and go there and secure her. Officers will arrive shortly to help. Do you understand?"

"No," said the understandably flustered librarian.

"Listen to me closely. Get a pen and a piece of paper right now," she ordered and managed to wait two full seconds before continuing. "Got them?"

"Yes? Is this a prank?"

"It's not a prank," Jessie said firmly, fighting the urge to yell. "Write the following down: Go find the security officer. Give him the name Hannah Dorsey. She's a senior. Tell him to find and secure her. She may be in danger. Give him the phone number that I'm about to give you and tell him to call me—Jessie Hunt."

The librarian eventually calmed down enough to repeat the instructions back to her. Then Jessie sent her on her way. Glancing at her phone, she saw a text from Ryan saying a unit was en route to the school and would be there in four minutes. Assuming her GPS was correct, she'd be there three minutes after that.

Three minutes. An eternity. What's the difference?

CHAPTER TWENTY SEVEN

Hannah was still pissed.

Jessie saw it immediately upon arriving in the security office, before the girl even said a word. And now, over an hour later, Hannah was clearly still seething.

In one sense, it was understandable. She had been dragged out of Calculus by the security officer without explanation, giving her and all her classmates the impression that she was being arrested. She had been ordered to the security office without any idea why she had to go. Two uniformed officers showed up moments later and stood guard outside the office until Jessie arrived.

She'd done her best to make it clear that her half-sister hadn't done anything wrong and that this was a safety measure for her own protection. But Hannah didn't care about that. She had been publicly embarrassed at a school she'd only been at for a week and a half. How was she supposed to try to reclaim a normal life if she couldn't even go to class without a crisis?

It was a fair question and as they waited in Jessie's car down the block from their destination, she tried her best to answer it. But Hannah wasn't satisfied. Telling a seventeen-year-old that her safety was a higher priority than her popularity didn't go over well. Telling her that returning to something resembling normalcy would occur in fits and starts got an enormous eye roll. Jessie feared how Hannah would react to her answer to the next question.

"What are we doing here?" she asked as they sat in Jessie's parked car on a quiet mid-Wilshire residential street.

"We're waiting for a colleague to arrive," Jessie answered.

"Is that what you're calling Ryan these days—a colleague? Did you two have a lovers' spat?"

"It's not Ryan," Jessie told her, refusing to be baited. "It's a man named Garland Moses. He's agreed to spend the afternoon with you while I look into the threat against you."

"Why can't we just go back to the apartment?" Hannah whined. "You've got so many locks and alarms and security codes, it's like frickin' Rikers Island. Aren't we safer there than at some shack on an unprotected city street?"

"We'll be able to go back there soon," Jessie assured her. "But for now, this is the best option. Garland Moses is one of the few people I totally trust. And with Kat on an impromptu trip to meet a charming deputy sheriff in Lake Arrowhead, he's the only one of those people currently available. So that's who you'll be hanging out with for the next few hours."

"Isn't he that old dude?"

"If by 'old,' you mean one of the most legendary forensic profilers in American history, then yeah, I guess he's on the older side."

"Yeah, old," Hannah reiterated. "How's that guy going to keep me safe?"

"Appearances can be deceiving, Hannah. That guy has tangled with more serial killers than you can name. You and I will never forget that night trapped with our psycho father. Garland Moses has been through half a dozen scrapes with guys like him. He's old but he's wily."

Just then, Moses pulled into his driveway. He got out of his beat up old VW bug and waved over at them.

"He drove here from the other direction and we're halfway down the block," Hannah noted. "How did he know this car was us?"

"Old guy instinct," Jessie replied as she started the car and pulled up in front of Moses's house.

The place wasn't a shack but it was on the smaller side. A quaint one-story, mid-century home, it looked out of place among the much larger, more modern houses that had taken over the block. The small porch out front looked like it had been built much more recently. Jessie couldn't explain why but she suspected Garland had done it himself.

"Hello, Ms. Hunt," he said with as close to warmth as he could muster. "And this must be the infamous Hannah Dorsey. I see the scowl is already in full effect."

"Hannah, this is Garland Moses," Jessie said, trying not to chuckle.

"Hi," Hannah said perfunctorily.

"Nice to meet you, Ms. Dorsey," he said. "Would you care to come in? That is, assuming you can handle the old man smell I can see you're obviously worried about."

"I'm okay with it," Hannah said, pretending to be hurt. "That is, assuming you don't mind a teenager cramping your style? I wouldn't want you to worry that I'm going to mess up your Russian nesting dolls or your collection of Victorian doilies."

Jessie was just opening her mouth to ream the girl out for her rudeness when she noticed Garland almost imperceptibly hold up his left hand to give her the "pause" signal. His body blocked Hannah's view so that only Jessie could see it. She held her tongue.

"I'll have you know," Garland said, with a sweetness she'd never heard in his tone before, "that I keep all my doilies under a glass case where they're safe from the grubby hands of unwashed pubescents. So you're all set."

Without waiting for a retort, he turned and led them to the front door. Once there, he punched a code into the keypad next to the doorbell. A metal cover pulled back to reveal several pieces of tech Jessie didn't recognize.

Garland bent down slightly and a device scanned his eyes. Then he placed his palm on a plate of glass below the scanner and watched as it apparently read his fingerprints. After that, he whispered something unintelligible into a speaker. Only then did the front door lock click.

"Wow," Hannah said, impressed. "That is some next level...stuff. Your security measures make Jessie's look like a joke."

"I have to keep those nesting dolls safe, don't I?" Garland replied as he welcomed them inside. When he closed the door after them, Jessie heard a series of locks slide into place. The process took about five seconds. She found the sound reassuring.

"So Ms. Dorsey..." Garland started.

"You can call me Hannah," she interrupted.

"So Hannah, why don't you head into the den? You can do your homework while your sister and I talk behind your back. Then I'll see what we have in the way of snacks. Sound good?"

Hannah nodded, clearly thrown and mildly amused by the unexpected quippiness of the old guy. When she was gone, Garland led Jessie to his office. He closed the door after she entered.

"It's soundproof," he assured her. "But I suspect she's going to get antsy soon. So I recommend you update me fast. I assume there's more to this than just the casual encounter you suggested I have with Hannah to profile her for you."

Jessie hadn't told Garland what was going on over the phone, only that she needed his advice and would like to get it somewhere he considered secure. He'd suggested his house and while she hadn't mentioned that Hannah would be with her, he didn't seem surprised that she was there.

"There *is* more to it than that. I won't bore you with all the details. And I don't want to put you in a compromising situation. But you know I've been investigating a murder in the Valley. You also know the bureau there has been very active in trying to close the case quickly. Now I've recently learned that the reason for this effort may have something to do with an LAPD higher-up who was involved with the victim."

"So the porn actress who was stabbed nine times was being paid for sex by someone of consequence in the department?" Garland asked.

Jessie looked at him, half-stunned and half-annoyed.

"If you knew everything already, why did you let me blather on?"

"I didn't know everything," he replied. "But I do try to keep up with what's going on case-wise. And I can draw inferences based on the information available to me. Care to explain how this turn of events has led you and your half-sister to my doorstep?"

"I don't think you need me to explain, Garland."

"No, probably not. I suspect you got a threatening note, or perhaps an e-mail or phone call recently, one suggesting that Hannah's safety might be at risk if you continue to pursue the case. Am I on the right track?"

"You know you are. It was a phone call. The voice was digitally masked."

"So, what exactly are you asking of me, Ms. Hunt?"

Jessie studied him, trying to discern how much she could pile on this man, who despite his reputation and skills was still a senior citizen with a lot to lose.

"I'd like you to keep an eye on Hannah while I'm out," she said.

"You're not asking me come up with a profile of her?" he asked.

Jessie shrugged.

"If, in the course of your time together, you glean worthwhile details about her that you deem shareable, I won't stop you."

Garland smiled.

"That was smooth," he noted. "Are you sure that's all you want? It feels like you're holding back."

"Well," she mused. "I don't want to put you in a difficult position."

"Too late."

"Okay, then. I'd love to get your thoughts on exactly what I'm up against here. Detective Hernandez seems to think this situation is . . . fraught."

"I would tend to agree with Detective Hernandez. If a high-level department official was involved with this girl, regardless of whether he actually killed her, he has a lot to lose if that information comes out. He is obviously using his considerable resources to ensure it doesn't, including tactics that are at best questionable, and after the threat you got, also illegal. If he thinks that you are likely to learn of and expose his involvement, there's no telling what other methods he'll employ to keep you quiet. You need to tread very carefully."

Jessie thought about this. Garland and Ryan seemed to be in sync about the threat she faced. But neither of them seemed to acknowledge what she saw as a fatal flaw in the "tread carefully" plan.

"Here's the problem with that," she said. "Even if I tread carefully or drop this case altogether, I don't see how that keeps me or Hannah safe long-term. What's to stop this guy, somewhere down the road when everything has settled, from taking me out just to be thorough? Even if he thinks I don't know his identity, he'll be paranoid that I'll discover it. I mean, as I long I'm out there, he's at risk, right? It's hard to imagine he'd put up with that."

"That's a legitimate concern," Garland conceded. "Of course, as we profilers so often have to, it's worth putting yourself in his position for a moment. He's had someone threaten your family member rather than actually harm her or you. That suggests that he doesn't want to escalate to the next level if he can avoid it. He doesn't want to push you too hard, whether he suspects you know who he is or not. He has to know that a détente with you, if it can be brokered, is preferable than having to take more dramatic action."

"What do you mean?" Jessie asked, though she sensed where he was headed.

"He has to know that harming your sister would likely have a boomerang effect and make you more likely to pursue him. Likewise, eliminating you would lead to all kinds of questions. There'd be an investigation of the cases you were investigating when you died and the information about him might come out anyway. And of course, Detective Hernandez, Captain Decker, and myself, among others, wouldn't just roll over if that happened. He'd be poking a hornet's nest with no guarantee that it would do him any good. He'd want to avoid that if at all possible. So he sends this not-so-veiled threat as a half-measure, hoping it will suffice."

"I get that, Garland," Jessie said, unconvinced. "But like I said, what about six months from now, long after I've dropped this case? What if I have an unfortunate fatal accident on the freeway? He could just bide his time and take me out down the line. Am I supposed to live the rest of my life worried that someone in the very department I work for might have me killed when I let my guard down?"

"It's a risk," Garland admitted unhelpfully.

"Yeah, well, I'm not sure it's a risk I'm willing to take. I don't see why I shouldn't take the more straightforward route."

"Which is?"

"Catch the killer. If this guy did it, he goes down. Not even his minions will defend a cop who stabbed an underage girl to death. If he didn't do it, maybe I can try to find a way to move on—accept that the killer is out of commission and let the lesser crimes go. Then maybe he'll let it go too."

Garland's expression suggested he wasn't convinced she was capable of that. She wasn't sure of it either.

"Then I guess you're right," he finally said. "The only way to get the upper hand and plot your own course is to catch the murderer, which was your plan all along anyway, correct?"

"Yep," she agreed. "I'm right back where I started. Solve the case. Then deal with the aftermath."

Chapter Twenty Eight

Jessie tried to be careful.

She had to assume that Commander Butters had people tailing her and any indication that she was still pursuing Michaela's killer could put her or Hannah at risk. So instead of meeting Ryan directly at their next stop in Culver City, she pulled into the covered parking structure of an outdoor mall down the block, took the elevator down to the first floor, and joined in with the mid-afternoon shopping crowd.

She entered a Japanese grocery store and walked briskly to the back storeroom. One employee gave her a suspicious glance but said nothing. Feigning confidence, she moved to the back exit, which opened onto an alley next to Washington Boulevard. She waited at the edge of the alley for a crowd to assemble at the crosswalk, and then joined them when the pedestrian sign turned green.

After quick stops into both a coffee shop and a bakery, she felt fairly confident that she'd evaded anyone following her. Even if she hadn't, there was nothing other than the Post-it linking the person she was about to see to the Penn case.

That person was Aaron Rose, a married corporate lawyer who worked out of a gleaming office tower in Culver City. The name matched the initials "A.R" from the Post-it. Of the two remaining photos in Michaela's envelope, his was the one FBI agent Jack Dolan had been able to identify.

The third man's photo wasn't in the system at all, which Dolan found odd, because, at the very least, his driver's license photo should have popped up. He couldn't explain it.

While he tried to solve that discrepancy, Jessie told Ryan to take a circuitous route and meet her at Rose's office to question him. She entered the office tower and headed straight for the service elevator. A security guard chased after her.

"Ma'am, you have to check in at the front desk," he ordered forcefully.

Jessie didn't stop until she was at the elevator door.

"I'm here to conduct an LAPD interview," she said, flashing her badge at him. "I'm trying to stay low profile so as to not cause a scene for your building's tenants. But if you prefer, I'll return to the lobby and sign in. Of course, I'll have to properly identify myself as a criminal profiler and ask for backup in case our person of interest tries to sneak out."

"Ma'am," the guard said, suddenly far less forceful, "we have our procedures."

"I was just trying to avoid a hassle for me and an embarrassment for you. But it's your call."

While the guard weighed whether it was worth it to stick to the letter of the law, Jessie waited. She preferred to go in this way and avoid being seen by any potential tail. But her gambit was already a partial success. If one of Butters's people had managed to stick with her and walked by or even entered the building, she was nowhere to be seen. The longer she could drag this encounter out, the better off she was, even if she did eventually have to sign in back in the lobby.

The guard opened his mouth, apparently having come to a decision. But before he could speak, Ryan rounded the corner.

"What's going on back here?" he demanded.

"Sir?" the guard said, now thoroughly flummoxed.

"Are you preventing my partner from entering the elevator?"

"Your partner?"

"Detective Hernandez, Homicide Special Section," Ryan said, holding out his badge uncomfortably close to the guard's face. "We're about to conduct an interview and it looks like you're interfering. Didn't you fill him in on this already, Hunt?"

"I did," Jessie said, adopting her best frustrated, impatient tone. "I told him I was trying to do this quietly to avoid a fuss for us or the building. But this gentleman was more interested in getting my John Hancock on his sign-in sheet. I told him I'd have to get way more official then—backup, squad car, sirens—the whole thing. But he doesn't seem to mind. So I guess we're lobby-bound."

"Hold on," the guard said desperately, clearly at a loss. His eyes were darting around like pinballs. "We can skip standard procedure this one time. But in the future, please at least consult with security before barreling down the hall."

Jessie and Ryan exchanged amused looks.

"You got it, pal," Ryan finally said. "Now may we please resume police business?"

The guard nodded. He turned his security key and hit the "up" button.

"What floor?" he asked.

"Seven," Jessie said.

"May I ask who you're visiting at least?"

"You can ask," Ryan said as the doors began to close. "But we can't tell you."

Once the doors shut completely and the elevator began moving, Jessie turned to him.

"You were a real jerk to that guy," she said, smiling.

"Are you kidding?" Ryan retorted, also grinning. "I could hear you yelling at him from the lobby. How do you think I knew where to find you?"

Jessie felt a strong urge to kiss him but fought it valiantly.

"Did anyone else seem interested?" she asked instead.

"You mean, could I tell if anyone had followed either of us? The answer is no. Of course, if they're really good I might have missed them. But I don't think I did."

The elevator pinged and the doors opened. They stepped out into the long hallway and made their way to the main entrance of the firm Conway, French & Sykes, where Aaron Rose worked. When they got to the door, they exchanged an excited glance.

"This could be our guy," Jessie whispered.

"Let's hope so," Ryan said. "I'd really rather our killer *not* be a department commander."

"We can dream," Jessie said, opening the door.

They walked up to the reception desk, where Jessie let Ryan do his thing. He was very good at it. He stood tall and square-shouldered in front of the harried girl hanging up the phone and flashed his badge as he spoke.

"I'm Detective Hernandez with the LAPD Homicide Special Section. This is Jessie Hunt. What's your name?"

"I'm Kaylee, sir."

"Hi, Kaylee," he said, smiling warmly. "We need to speak to Aaron Rose about a pressing matter. Please take us to him."

"Of course," the receptionist said, trying to stay cool. "Just let me call him and let him know you're here."

"No thank you," Ryan said firmly. "We'd like you to take us to him directly right now; no need to call."

Kaylee looked torn between her typical instructions and her new ones. But Ryan's forceful but polite demand won out pretty easily. She nodded and motioned for them to follow as she walked down the hall.

"Remember," Ryan whispered to Jessie as walked, "we don't have approval for any of this. So let's not back him in a corner that makes him lash out and start making calls. If we're not sure it's him, we need to tread carefully."

Jessie nodded in agreement. She'd already been through a variation of this with the Zellers, though she doubted that a corporate lawyer like Rose would be as amenable to helping as they were. If he was resistant to talking, it would be hard to pry details from him without creating some anxiety in the man. The question was how much was too much.

Kaylee arrived at Rose's office door and knocked.

"Busy," came a loud, nasally shout from inside.

"Open the door," Ryan said quietly.

Kaylee nodded and then actually physically closed her eyes as she opened the door. In the far corner of the room, behind a large desk, was a balding man with an aggressive comb-over.

He stood up and Jessie realized he couldn't have been more than about five foot five. His skin was pale in a way that suggested he didn't get outside often. He wore a tucked-in dress shirt and tie and it was clear that he was in good shape, with a muscular, wiry frame. As proof of his workout devotion, an elliptical machine stood in the other corner of the room.

"What the hell, Kaylee?" he bellowed. "I said I was busy, goddammit!"

"I'm sorry Mr. Rose but these . . ."

"That's okay, Kaylee," Ryan interrupted. "You can go. We've got it from here."

He stepped inside and shut the door behind Jessie after she entered.

"Who do you think you are?" Rose demanded, his eyes blazing.

"I think that I'm Detective Ryan Hernandez of the Los Angeles Police Department," he replied calmly. "And I think this is Jessie Hunt, who is one of our top criminal profilers. I suggest you hang up the phone, Mr. Rose. We have a few questions for you."

The lawyer did hang up but didn't look much more chastened than before.

"You've got five minutes," he said sharply.

Jessie felt her whole body tighten up and saw Ryan's forearms flex involuntarily as well. She wanted to crush the guy but reminded herself that going straight to eleven on the pressure meter wouldn't be the wisest move. Rose was clearly trying to bait them. They couldn't let him.

"Mr. Rose," she said, choosing to ignore his comment, "what kind of clients do you represent?"

The man's expression went from combative to smug.

"Why? Are you looking for representation? I doubt you could afford me on your salary."

"But you don't represent individuals much anyway, right?" she said, unfazed. "I thought your clients were mostly big-time corporate accounts. Do I have that wrong?"

"No," Rose replied, smirking. "I represent some of most notable companies in the L.A. area, a who's who of the who's who. Are you alleging impropriety on one of their parts? If so, this is pretty unorthodox, just busting into my office like this. Why don't you make a proper appointment and I'll have my girl try to fit you in? My schedule is jam-packed today."

Jessie half-glanced at Ryan, letting him know that now that Rose wasn't so on the defensive, she was going to drop the hammer.

"What can you tell us about a woman named Missy Mack?" she asked without preamble.

Rose's smugness immediately disappeared, if only for a moment.

"Before you answer, sir," Ryan added, "you should probably ask yourself why we would be here in your office asking you this question. I'll give you a hint. It's not just out of curiosity."

Rose's eyes narrowed and Jessie could see him strategizing his response.

"Are you asking if I know her? Because of course I know Missy," he said. "You obviously know that. She's an actress I've gone out with on a few occasions. Is that illegal now?"

"Gone out with?" Ryan repeated.

"Sure. We had a few meals together. Sometimes we'd splurge and get an expensive bottle of champagne. She's a fun girl."

"So you'd buy a really expensive bottle of champagne for your dates with Missy?" Ryan asked.

"Actually, because I'm so busy, I'd usually just give Missy the cash to buy it for us."

"Cash," Ryan repeated.

"Of course," Rose replied as if it was obvious. "You think a liquor store would just let some random girl use my credit card to buy champagne worth hundreds of dollars? Cash was much easier."

"So just to be clear," Ryan reviewed, sarcasm dripping off him, "you would give Missy hundreds of dollars in cash and she would use it to buy expensive bottles of champagne for the two of you to drink together."

"That's exactly right, Detective," Rose answered with a broad smile on his face.

"And did Missy ever find creative ways to thank you for your generosity?" Ryan pressed.

"Thank me? No. You don't have to be coy, Detective. If you're asking if our evenings ever ended in sexual encounters, then the answer is yes. But I assure you, that was simply two people enjoying a few stimulating evenings together."

"No connection to the cash you gave her?" Ryan asked.

"None whatsoever; never entered my mind."

"Aren't you married, Mr. Rose?" Jessie asked, making a hard conversational turn.

"I am."

"How does your wife feel about your dates with Missy?"

Rose smiled even wider, revealing coffee-stained teeth.

"I'm sure she'd be unhappy if she was to ever find out. Do you plan on telling her, Ms. Hunt? Is adultery now a crime in this state?"

"No. But providing alcohol to a minor is."

"Oh dear," Rose said mockingly, reaching to his neck to clutch imaginary pearls. "The horror! If you plan to toss me in lockup for that, be my guest. And before you shut the cell door, I'll have my firm slap a suit against you for everything under the sun—harassment, false imprisonment, police intimidation."

Jessie beamed back at him.

"You realize by minimizing this, you're also tacitly acknowledging that you were having sex with a minor. With that and the alcohol charge, things are really starting to add up here."

"Ms. Hunt," Rose said, unruffled, "you are making unwarranted assumptions. I never confirmed that I knew Missy was underage. It's not like I asked her for ID. I learned about her because she's an actress working in the adult film industry. I thought you had be an *adult* to do that. If she's a minor, that's news to me."

Jessie didn't plan to let him off that easy.

"So you're telling me that as a competent attorney with a thriving career, you didn't do your due diligence before getting involved with this girl?"

Rose seemed unbothered by the question.

"Do you ask to check the licenses of your dates for their birthdays, Ms. Hunt? Come on now, what is this really about? I know you didn't come all the way here and bust into my office to give me a hard time over unprovable charges."

Jessie glanced at Ryan, letting him know she thought the time had come. His half-nod indicated he agreed.

"Missy's dead," he said.

Aaron Rose's already pale face turned ashen. When he finally regained the ability to speak, he croaked a question.

"What happened?"

"She was murdered, Mr. Rose," Ryan said. "Are you asserting that you know nothing about this?"

"No," he said, the attitude gone. "I mean, we have a standing date every other Thursday, including tomorrow. She usually calls the day of to reconfirm. When did this happen?"

"Monday night. And her real name is Michaela Penn, by the way."

"She never told me that," he whispered, more to himself than to them.

"Where were you two evenings ago, Mr. Rose?" Jessie asked brusquely, refusing to give him time to organize his thoughts.

"What?" he asked distractedly. "Oh, right, of course."

He sat back down and moved his computer mouse around. After several seconds, he looked up, both relieved and distraught.

"Monday night, right? I was at a bar association banquet. It ran until ten thirty. Then my wife and I went home to relieve the babysitter. I was in bed by midnight."

Jessie felt like a deflated balloon but tried to hide her disappointment. Ryan, more experienced with this sort of thing, did a better job of it.

"We'll need the babysitter's number," he said matter-of-factly, "as well as contact information for the bar event."

"Not a problem," Rose said, writing down the numbers as he spoke. He was sounding increasingly confident. "I can also give you access to the security camera footage at my house. It will show our return home and when I left the next morning."

"We'll need it," Ryan said. "And until we can verify your alibi, I wouldn't recommend any travel, Mr. Rose."

"Of course not," the lawyer replied, not yet back to full smarm but getting there quickly.

"We'll be in touch," Ryan said.

They were almost out the door when Rose called out to them.

"Do you know where the funeral is being held?" he asked. "I obviously can't go. But I'd like to send flowers."

"We don't have that information," Ryan said. "But I'll let you know when I find out."

As they walked out, Jessie felt a pang in her chest. What kind of funeral would Michaela get? Could her father even afford one? The fact that none of these things had occurred to her until just now filled her with guilt.

And the realization that Aaron Rose had thought of it before her filled her with shame.

CHAPTER TWENTY NINE

He wasn't that bad for an old guy.

Hannah would never admit it out loud. But she actually got a kick out of Garland Moses, whom she'd taken to calling the snarky geriatric. She didn't use the term out loud, but every time she thought of it, she couldn't help but grin.

Though he'd told her when she and Jessie had first arrived that she should go to the den to finish her homework, he hadn't followed up on it. After she described how she'd been dragged out of her classroom, he smiled ruefully before speaking.

"I think that gives you a free pass for at least one day. Why don't we play Connect Four instead? It's not calculus but it's kind of math-y."

So that's what they did for the next few hours—played games and ate chocolate chip cookies. Hannah could tell the guy was smart but there wasn't anything about him that would have led her to believe that he'd hunted down multiple serial killers. The man didn't even seem interested in brushing his hair. When they got bored with the games, he invited her out to his backyard to help feed his koi fish. They sat on deck chairs and tossed food pellets into the small pond.

"So your sister says you just started at this—what did she call it—therapeutic school last week," he said. "What exactly is a therapeutic high school anyway?"

Hannah laughed, mostly because she often asked herself the same question.

"Officially? It's a special learning environment that caters to students facing extreme emotional and psychological challenges."

"And unofficially?" Garland asked.

"It's a way station for screw-ups."

"Screw-ups or the screwed up?" he pressed.

She thought about it for a second. The question hinted at a distinction she'd never really considered before.

"Both, I guess. There are some kids there who were abused or victims of violent crime—rapes, beatings—stuff like that. They didn't do anything wrong. They just have massive PTSD because of it. But most people are there because of something they did. There's a girl who broke into a convenience store to pay for her Oxy habit. One guy beat up his teacher. This other girl with impulse control issues keeps hitting on the teachers, like all of them."

"So which one are you?" he wondered. "Screw-up or screwed up?"

She rolled her eyes even as she smiled at him.

"Oh man, sorry. I know you're just making conversation but you sound like my therapist. And since you and I don't have doctor/patient confidentiality, maybe I'll pass on the oversharing. I don't need you ratting me out to Jessie."

"Fair enough," Garland said. "We can just feed the fish."

They did that for a few minutes. The silence was surprisingly comfortable. Then Garland spoke up again.

"What makes you think it would be ratting you out to tell Jessie whether you considered yourself screwed up or a screw-up? Is that some secret information?"

"No," she admitted. "But I know she worries about me enough already. I don't need her fixating on my sense of self-worth too."

Garland chuckled softly to himself.

"What?" she asked, irked.

"Nothing," he said, then changed his mind. "It's just that, don't you think she's already doing that all the time? I mean, no offense but your birth father was a serial killer who tortured both his daughters. Anyone who doesn't doubt themselves after learning that family tidbit would be ... screwed up. She's going to worry about your well-being, no matter what. My telling her you have a messed-up self-image isn't going to come as a shock to her."

"What's your point?"

"My point," he said, not looking at her but at one of the fish swimming back and forth, "is that you're obviously screwed up. No sane person wouldn't be after what you've been through. The question is: why do you consider yourself a screw-up too?"

"I never said I did," Hannah protested.

"But you do feel that way, right? Otherwise you wouldn't have responded like there was something to be ashamed of. You can't help being screwed up. But if you're a screw-up, that's kind of on you, right?"

Hannah felt the heat rise to her cheeks.

"Are you blaming me for what happened to me?" she demanded.

"No. But I think you are."

"Where do you get that from?"

"I think you feel guilty about your mistakes before your parents died, about the bad choices you made. I think you feel guilty, as if everything that happened to you, to them, was a result of whatever you were doing that you didn't want them to know about."

Hannah stood up and looked down at him. She knew he was intentionally poking at her, trying to get a rise. But she couldn't stop herself from responding.

"What didn't I want them to know about?" she asked accusatorily.

"I couldn't possibly know," he said. "Probably nothing; maybe sneaking off to a keg party in the woods, smoking weed in the bathroom during lunch, letting that guy with the tattoos feel you up behind the bleachers, stealing makeup from the department store. That kind of thing."

"You think I did all that stuff?"

"I don't know what choices you made. But I think you feel like you were punished for making those kinds of choices, like you deserve what's happened to you, like your parents paid the price that you owed."

"You're wrong," she said, pretending not to notice the tears that burned in her eyes.

"Probably," he conceded. "I usually am. Just out of curiosity, what exactly am I wrong about this time around?"

"You're wrong that I feel guilty about what happened to them," she said, her voice quiet as she spoke aloud for the first time what she'd thought silently many times before. "I feel guilty because I *don't* feel bad about what happened to them. I know I should. But in the spot where the sadness and the guilt should go, there's nothing. I don't feel anything at all, at least not for them."

She couldn't help but notice that Garland had stopped feeding the fish.

CHAPTER THIRTY

They didn't have much time.

Between the Zellers interview, the Aaron Rose interrogation, and all their sneaking around, it was bound to get back to someone that they weren't spending all their time on the Ristore tennis murder.

Once word got out, there were likely two outcomes. Decker shut them down and took their badges. Or worse, Commander Butters and his minions came after them. But they were committed now. The only way out of this, both professionally and personally, was to find out who killed Michaela Penn.

"Do you still have the GPS data from Michaela's calls?" Jessie asked Ryan as they drove back from Culver City to the station in his car. They'd left hers in the parking structure.

"Yeah," he said, handing it over. "What are you thinking?"

"Now that we know three of Michaela's clients, I was hoping we could find some connection among them that might lead us to the other one listed on her Post-it list. We still don't know who D.K. is."

Ryan shook his head.

"Normally I'd suggest we give the data to the tech team," he said. "But I'm sure Butters has tagged his name in the system. If we include him on any list, he'll know and we'll have shown our hand."

"So we'll have to do it old school," Jessie said, looking over Michaela's location data. "It actually shouldn't be that hard. The girl led a pretty provincial life, all things considered. In the last month, she rarely went more than ten miles from her apartment; lots of trips to work, the grocery store, the mall, the movies. She almost never left her little corner of the Valley."

"That makes sense," Ryan said. "It's the area she knew best and probably where she felt safest."

Jessie was only half-listening. One of her own comments had given her an idea. She began flipping back among different days, making notations on the sheet as she went along.

"What is it?" Ryan asked, watching her out of the corner of his eye as he drove.

"It just occurred to me how regular her habits were. I mean, she truly almost never left her neck of the woods. I count only eleven total trips over the hills into L.A. proper in the last four weeks."

"For an independent teenage girl who was making serious money, that is surprising," Ryan agreed.

Jessie started tallying up the visits.

"Yeah, I'm starting to think she may have *only* left the Valley to meet clients. Two of the trips appear to be to Aaron Rose's Culver City office, both on Thursdays, just like he said. Two more trips are to the Zellers's house. Those stop about a week ago, right around the time they broke things off. There are also two trips to a Travelodge motel in the Adams district."

"That would probably be her meeting Butters," Ryan said. "The department has a deal with the chain for reduced, sometimes even waived rates. And the location you're looking at is about halfway between LAPD headquarters and where Butters lives in Hancock Park. I can't prove it, but it fits."

"Okay," Jessie said, making a note on the paper. "That leaves five more times she left the valley in the last month. If we could determine where she was going, maybe we could identify other clients."

Ryan sighed from the driver's seat.

"What?" she said. Something was obviously bothering him.

"Nothing," he said, though it clearly wasn't. "Tell me what you found."

She decided not to push him and returned to the list.

"Of the five other times she came to the city, one was to Hollywood and one was to Santa Monica. Both stops were in large shopping districts. They might be dead ends. But the three other visits were all to an address in Beverly Hills, on Wilshire just off Rodeo Drive. It looks like it's a medical office tower. Three times in a month? That sounds like a regular client to me. We should check it out."

"An entire medical building?" Ryan asked, sounding exasperated. "Come on. It's one thing if it's a home but there are likely dozens of offices in that tower. How do you propose we narrow it down?"

"The same way we would have done if we had gone to Aaron Rose's building without knowing he was the client. We'd look at the tenants and see if any names match the initials on the Post-it."

"But Rose wasn't listed in the building directory," he reminded her. "Only the name of the firm was. Without knowing his name ahead of time from that photo, we would never have found him."

Jessie felt his frustration seeping into her.

"Well, what do you suggest?" she asked snippily.

He looked over at her, reluctant to answer.

"You're not going to like it," he said.

"Don't let that stop you."

"Okay. Maybe we *don't* go to Beverly Hills. Maybe we stop running around, putting our careers at risk, for what feels like a wild goose chase."

"I don't get it," she protested. "Less than twenty minutes ago, we agreed that the only way to save our careers was to solve this."

"Right. But that only works if there's something to solve. All this hunting around that we're doing doesn't guarantee that we're going to find anything other than more people who paid Michaela for sex. As bad as that is, it's not murder."

"What are you getting at?" she asked, sensing she didn't like where he was going.

"Maybe this case has already been solved. Maybe the person who stabbed Michaela Penn to death is already in jail. Nothing we've uncovered so far, not even what Costabile has done to protect Commander Butters, has suggested anyone other than Pete Vasquez did this. He had her laptop, the one stolen from her apartment. That is hard evidence. And he has no alibi, unless you're convinced by his claim of drinking in a park alone. Maybe this case is like the tennis coach thing. Maybe the most likely suspect really is guilty of the crime."

Jessie sat quietly, processing everything he'd said. None of it was unreasonable. In fact, objectively, she was the one being unreasonable by pursuing this without anything definitive to suggest she was on the right track. And yet, she couldn't let it go.

"I just have this feeling, Ryan," she said softly.

"I thought you told me you were trying to work less off feelings and more off the evidence. Isn't that what they emphasized in the FBI Academy training you did?"

"You're going to throw that back at me now?" she asked, her voice rising in irritation.

Ryan didn't respond. Instead, he pulled over to the side of the road. He put the car in park and looked over at her.

"Yes, I'm going to throw that back at you, because we're talking about both our careers here. We can't just count on some feeling you have, no matter how much you trust it."

"But it's not just that and you know it," she reminded him. "My sister was threatened by someone. That wasn't imaginary. And you're the one who got the call from Chatty Cathy that started this whole thing."

Ryan sighed heavily. It made Jessie feel like she was an obstinate child he was humoring. She didn't like it. He got out of the car and closed the door. She did the same, then walked over to where he stood looking down at the asphalt road.

"Yes," he said when he'd calmed down enough to speak, "I got the call. But I already told you, that could easily have just been about Butters being sexually involved with Michaela. We don't have any credible reason to suggest it was more than that. And as frustrating as it is that he might skate on this, we're kind of stuck."

"But what if Chatty Cathy thought there was more to it than just paying for sex?" she pressed.

"I'm all ears if you have any evidence to back that up. Otherwise, it's just supposition, and suicidal supposition at that."

"Can't you just trust me on this?" she pleaded.

"I do trust you, Jessie. But despite what you may believe, this isn't about you. Not everything is."

She stared at him, briefly struck dumb.

"What the hell does that mean?" she finally demanded.

"It means you have a habit of making yourself the center of the universe," he told her, not backing down. "There always has to be a conspiracy and you always have to be the one to uncover it, to solve it. You're always at a fever pitch. It's like you won't slow down for anything else, not even us."

Again, Jessie was briefly stunned into silence. But only briefly.

"How did a murder investigation suddenly become a test of our relationship?"

"How can it not be?" he challenged.

She was about to come back at him, to let him know just what a cheap shot she thought that was, when she saw his attention focus on something behind her and his eyes open wide. She turned around to determine what had distracted him, to see a gray sedan barreling down on them, veering dangerously from the next lane over.

Before she could react, she felt Ryan's hands on her hips as he physically lifted her and tossed her onto the hood of his car, diving up right after her.

The sedan scraped the edge of his car as it continued down the road, unabated. Just before it made a sharp right onto the next street, Jessie noted that the car had no license plate.

"Are you okay?" Ryan asked as he rolled off the now-crushed hood of his car.

"I think so," she said, easing off herself. "Thanks."

He nodded.

"Did you notice that the driver wore a mask?" he asked.

"No," she said. "But I saw that the car was unmarked. Between the two, it's hard to believe that was an accidental hit and run."

"I'd agree it's a stretch."

"So what do we do now?" she asked.

"Look," he replied. "We've obviously got some stuff to work out. But this thing has escalated from just your gut feelings. Someone tried to take us out. I don't know who. But until this gets resolved, we're clearly not safe."

"So how do you want to resolve it?"

"I guess we're going to Beverly Hills."

CHAPTER THIRTY ONE

They were almost there when they got the call.

"Don't answer it," Jessie implored.

"I have to," Ryan said. "It's from the chief's office. There's a standing policy for every cop in the department. If you get a direct call from this number, you answer it immediately, no matter what."

He pushed "accept" and put the call on speaker.

"This is Detective Ryan Hernandez," he said, trying not to sound intimidated.

"Hold for Chief Laird," a female voice said.

Before Ryan could reply, another voice came on the line.

"Is this Hernandez?" a booming, gravelly voice demanded.

"It is, sir," Ryan replied.

"Is Hunt with you?"

"Yes sir."

"I understand that you were removed from a case you were working in tandem with Valley Bureau, is that correct?"

"Yes sir," Ryan conceded.

"I further understand that you were reassigned to a new case by your captain this morning. Is that also correct?"

"Yes sir," Ryan repeated.

"It has been brought to my attention that, despite your removal and a clear warning that pursuing the case would result in disciplinary action, you have continued to investigate. Is that correct?"

"Where did you hear that, sir?" Jessie asked, trying not to sound too accusatory and mostly failing.

"That's not your concern, Ms. Hunt. The more important question is: is it true?"

Ryan looked at Jessie, shrugging resignedly.

"It is, sir," he said.

"All right then. Let me be clear. You are both suspended with pay pending a formal disciplinary hearing. You have thirty minutes to return to your station and turn in your badges and weapons. If you haven't done so by that time, your suspension will be without pay and you may be brought up on charges. Are we clear?"

"Yes sir," Ryan said, shaking his head at Jessie, who had opened her mouth to protest.

"All right then," Chief Laird said. "Good day."

The line went dead just as they pulled up in front of the Wilshire Medical Center.

"So I guess we're turning around then?" Jessie asked playfully.

"Is that what you're thinking?" Ryan asked, his eyebrows raised.

"Well, let's see. Since we started on this case, members of the organization we work for have covered up details about the death of an underage porn actress, likely threatened my sister's safety, surveilled our movements, and quite possibly tried to hit us with an unmarked car. I think I'm gonna take a pass on going back to the station. I think I'm gonna stick around here and see what I can find out. You?"

"Considering I was being sarcastic," he replied, grinning widely, "I think I'll hang out here too."

"Then it's settled. Let's get in there."

Forty-five minutes later, they still had nothing.

There were a total of five doctors in the building's lobby directory who had the initials D.K. but none of them matched the photo. It was possible that D.K. was someone other than a doctor but that seemed less likely, considering the cost of Michaela's services.

After going through the list, Ryan suggested that maybe the building was simply slow to add recent doctor names to the board. As a result, they'd been reduced to checking the list of doctor names outside each office individually in the hope that they'd come across one who hadn't been listed in the lobby directory. When they reached the sixth and final floor, Ryan showed Jessie a text he'd just gotten from Captain Decker. It read:

We have passed insubordination. Your phone shows that you are in Beverly Hills. You were supposed to be at the station fifteen minutes ago. Captain Laird is demanding your arrest. I am en route to your location. Turn yourselves in to avoid additional penalties.

"Well," she said. "We're on the top floor. If we don't have luck here, we may as well turn ourselves in. At least we can cut through traffic if we're in a squad car with sirens, right?"

"You are a ray of light, Jessie Hunt," Ryan said, smiling through his anxiety.

"Remember that when they're slapping the cuffs on you," she replied.

They took opposite sides of the hallway, checking the names on placards for a match. Jessie looked at the four doctors listed outside Wilshire Plastic Surgery Associates. When she got to the third name, she stopped in her tracks. After a moment, she quickly typed it into Google. When the image came up, she stared at it for several seconds.

"Ryan," she called out as she checked additional images for the doctor, "can you come over here?"

He walked over and she showed him the photo on her phone. Then she pulled out the picture of the sleeping guy from Michaela's picture.

"Hard to be sure," Ryan said. "But they definitely look similar. What's his name?"

"Dr. Richard Kallas," Jessie said. "I wonder if he goes by the nickname Dick."

Ryan's eyes lit up.

"D.K," he breathed. "I'm thinking maybe we should have a chat with the good doctor."

"Me too," Jessie said.

Ryan started to open the door but Jessie stopped him for a moment so she could get out her phone. She typed a message to Decker and before Ryan could stop her she hit "send."

"Why did you do that?" he demanded.

"Gut feeling," she said and gave him a wink.

Shaking his head, he opened the door and followed her in.

The receptionist looked up, startled.

"Oh, I'm sorry. We're closed for the day. I guess I forgot to lock the door. But you can make an appointment online. We have openings in about four months."

Jessie looked at the clock. It read 5:11 p.m.

"We're not here for a consultation," she said. "We need to speak to Dr. Kallas."

"I'm afraid Dr. Kallas isn't available," she said impatiently. "But as I said, you can…"

"We're with the LAPD," Ryan interrupted. "Is he in his office?"

The receptionist glanced down the hall uncertainly.

"Yes," she said. "He's finishing patient charts."

"Why don't you take us to him?" Ryan asked, though it wasn't really a request.

The receptionist nodded and led the way down the hall. As he had on the way to Aaron Rose's office, Ryan gave Jessie a friendly reminder.

"I know we're not worried about it getting out that we're still investigating the case. That ship has sailed. But don't forget, even if this guy did sleep with Michaela, that doesn't mean he killed her. Let's try not to add any lawsuits for defamation to our pending disciplinary action."

Jessie nodded her understanding, if not her agreement. She wasn't worried about lawsuits right now, just getting to the truth.

The receptionist stopped outside the last, slightly ajar door at the end of the hall and knocked softly.

"Yes?" someone said in a soothing voice.

"Dr. Kallas, it's Maya. I know you're working on charts but you have some visitors who need to speak with you."

"We'll take it from here," Ryan said, pushing the door open and stepping inside.

Jessie followed close behind. As she entered she took a deep breath and pushed all the chaos of the day out of her mind. She needed to focus completely to determine if Richard Kallas was just a scumbag or something far worse.

Kallas stood up as they entered. He had an untroubled smile on his face. The second she saw him, Jessie knew he was the same man from Michaela's photo. Kallas was handsome in a creepy, manufactured way.

His brown hair was shockingly full and vibrant for a man who looked to be in his early forties, without a hint of gray. Jessie suspected it was aided by a transplant and colored often. His skin was golden and his teeth were brilliant white. He looked to be in great shape, with a trim waist and muscles that strained at his dress shirt.

Behind him on the wall, Jessie saw a collection of photos from marathons and Iron Man competitions, just above a series of what appeared to be vintage scalpels and surgical blades, some of which looked more like weapons than precision tools. In some of the pictures, his face looked dramatically different from the man standing before them now.

Part of it was simple aging. But part of it was also due to artificial attempts to defy age. The real-life Kallas had smooth skin and no visible wrinkles near his eyes or on his forehead, both of which made him look weirdly like a plastic Ken doll.

His nose and chin were different from some of the photos as well. Both had been sculpted. The chin was broader and squarer and the nose was smaller and sharper than before. The skin below his cheekbones looked tightened as well, giving him the permanent appearance of someone sucking them in. Even his ears looked slightly different, as if they'd been tweaked so as to not stick out as far.

No wonder Agent Dolan's FBI people hadn't been able to match the photo she gave him to the man in front of them now. Being asleep in that picture couldn't have made it easy. But in addition, if Kallas had most of the work on his face done recently, after his driver's license photo was taken, it might be hard for even a computer make the match.

"What can I do for you?" he asked politely. "I gather you're not here for a consultation?"

"Why do you say that?" Jessie asked.

Kallas smiled even more broadly than before. He glanced over at Maya, who was hovering by the door.

"You can go home, Maya. I'll close up," he said, turning back to Jessie and Ryan. "Because neither of you seem to need much work...yet. You are both gorgeous physical specimens. It looks like you stepped out of a fashion magazine, or at the very least, a department store catalogue."

"Thanks," Ryan muttered.

"Don't get me wrong," Kallas said, stepping around his desk to get a closer look at them. "The gentleman has a few forehead wrinkles that could be easily buffed out. But at your age, they come across as distinguished. Maybe come see me in five years. And the lady looks shockingly good considering what—and forgive me for saying this—is clearly some recent trauma."

"Why do you say that?" Jessie asked, wondering if plastic surgeons and profilers shared some of the same skill set.

"Well, the lines around the eyes are more pronounced than one would expect in a woman your age. I'm guessing you're about thirty. But their configuration suggests stress and lack of sleep rather than normal skin degradation. You've been through a lot, especially recently. But still, I wouldn't recommend doing anything for another half a decade or so. It would look desperate at this early stage. I could do something about the scars though."

"The scars?"

He nodded at her forearms, which were marked by multiple confrontations with both serial killers and more everyday criminals.

"Those are easy," he said. "The one near your throat would require more work. It's quite angry."

Jessie forced herself not to cover the scar with her hand. The handiwork of her father and a hunting knife when she was six, it ran along her collarbone from the base of her neck all the way to her right shoulder. Other than psychological distress, it was the one enduring gift he'd left her with. Kallas's casual mention of it made her skin crawl.

"I'm good, thanks," she said, trying not to sound curt. "Tell me, Dr. Kallas, do you go by Richard or Dick?"

"Well, that strikes me as quite a personal question. I'll answer if you tell me if you prefer Jessie or Jessica?"

Despite her best efforts, Jessie couldn't stop from gasping slightly.

"How do you know who I am? I haven't introduced myself."

"Which you must admit is a bit rude," Kallas said. "But don't worry. I'm not some mind-reader. I'm a law-abiding, well-informed citizen. And you, Ms. Hunt, are in the news quite a bit, a law enforcement celebrity of sorts. It'd be hard not to recognize you. I don't recognize the gentleman but I'm going to assume he is also some kind of cop. Maybe an FBI agent? Federal marshal? So many choices."

"This is Detective Ryan Hernandez, LAPD Central Station. And to answer your question, I go by Jessie."

"Ah, then let me answer yours," Kallas said, leaning back to rest his backside on the edge of his desk. "Professionally, it's Richard. My dear departed mother went with Dickie, which was not my favorite. Friends use Dick, sometimes with more enthusiasm than I would prefer. Are we going to be friends, Jessie?"

"I kind of doubt it, Richard," she told him.

"That is truly disappointing," he replied sadly.

But the cold, calculating look in his eyes suggested he already viewed them as foes.

Chapter Thirty Two

Jessie felt a shiver run down her spine.

She knew she wasn't supposed to depend on her gut to the exclusion of all else. But something told her the man in front of them was very dangerous. It was nothing overt. But in a way she couldn't quite verbalize, his manner was just...off. That didn't mean he was a killer. But he definitely wasn't, as he described himself, just a "law-abiding, well-informed citizen."

"Are you married, Richard?" she asked, trying to shake him out of the cockiness he clearly felt here at the home field of his office.

His brow furrowed slightly, probably as much as was possible considering all the Botox in his forehead.

"Sadly no," he admitted. "Three engagements but never made it to the altar. Why do you ask? Are you in the market?"

"I'm afraid not," she said. "I'm spoken for."

"Of course you are," Kallas replied. "How could you not be? I mean, despite the incarcerated ex-husband and the serial killer daddy, you're still quite a catch, though I imagine the emotional support required of your partner would be significant."

Jessie managed not to glance at Ryan. Kallas continued.

"So, if you're not here looking for a date, I have to wonder the reason for this visit. Forgive my curiosity but I've had two law enforcement types in my office after work hours for several minutes now and I'm still not clear why. Care to share?"

"Of course," Ryan said, taking a slight step forward so that he was physically between Kallas and Jessie. "We have a few questions for you about a woman named Missy Mack. Are you familiar with her?"

Without any hesitation, Kallas smiled and gave a soft chuckle. It was not the reaction Jessie expected.

"Do you mean Michaela Penn?" he asked. "Of course I know her."

"In what capacity?" Ryan asked.

"Well, I can't get into too many specifics because of HIPAA requirements, but she's a patient."

"She's a patient of yours?" Jessie asked incredulously.

"Technically, she's a *potential* surgical patient. She'd come in for several consultations but we hadn't come to any final determination about actions going forward."

"What kind of actions?" Jessie pressed.

"As I said, privacy regulations prevent me from getting specific," Kallas replied, adopting an apologetic tone. "You'd need a waiver from Ms. Penn before I could speak about her care."

Ryan glanced over at Jessie. She knew what was coming and trained all her attention on Kallas.

"Michaela Penn is dead," Ryan said bluntly.

Kallas's permanent smile disappeared.

"What?" he said.

"Michaela Penn was murdered two days ago. So according to HIPAA disclosure provisions, you are able to share her information with law enforcement."

Kallas shook his head, not so much in refusal but because he seemed not to have fully processed the information.

"I'm sorry," he said. "You said Michaela's dead?"

"That's correct," Ryan said. "When did you see her last?"

"I don't know," he said, putting his hand to his forehead and rubbing it vigorously. "I think it was recently. I'd have to check my records to be sure."

"Go ahead," Ryan said. "We'll wait."

Jessie watched Kallas closely as he returned to his desk. While there was no "correct" way to respond to the news of someone's death, he was behaving within the normal range of expected reactions.

And yet, Jessie got the sense that he was play-acting. She just couldn't discern whether that was because he didn't really care about Michaela much and felt like he had to fake it or because he was involved in her death.

The doctor sat down at his desk and punched a few keys and looked at his screen.

"It looks like she was in just this last Monday, in the afternoon. She was on the verge of deciding whether to have a procedure done."

"What procedure was that?" Jessie asked.

"Um, okay," he said, no longer concerned with privacy claims. "As you clearly know, Michaela was an adult film actress. She was looking into breast augmentation. She thought it might be good for her career."

"That's why she was coming here?" Ryan asked, disbelieving.

"Yes, of course. I consulted with her on three occasions. She told me that she planned to make a final decision this week so that I could schedule surgery if she pulled the trigger. Why else would she come here?"

Had she not seen the photo of Kallas asleep, she would have found his feigned innocence borderline convincing. He was good. The question was whether his deception was to hide an inappropriate relationship with a patient or something more.

"Dr. Kallas," Jessie said, staring him in the eyes. "That's the problem. You see, we know that Michaela wasn't just your patient, if she was ever your patient at all. And the fact that you're not being straight with us about it can't help but make us doubt everything else you've told us. Would you like to try again?"

"Excuse me?" he said, the sadness on his face now replaced by self-righteous anger. "What exactly are you alleging?"

"Look, Dr. Kallas," Ryan said, giving Jessie his patented "cool it" glare, "we understand that you're in a precarious position here. But the more forthcoming you can be with us now, the less messy it has to get later. We're looking for information, not confrontation. So how about telling us the whole story about your relationship with Michaela? I can't promise that you'll emerge from this unscathed. But we're looking for a killer, not a doctor who let his fantasies get in the way of his professionalism. Once we can eliminate you as the former, we can find a way to deal with you as the latter. What do you say?"

Kallas continued to look indignant.

"I say that this conversation is over. The next one you have will be with my attorney. I hope the police department's insurance policy covers the damage these false allegations could do to my business, because I'm going to clean it out."

"We have a picture," Jessie said sharply.

"What?" Kallas said, his voice still resentful, but his eyes closer to panicked.

"You heard me," Jessie repeated, enjoying him try not to squirm. "There is a photo that does not comport with your description of your association with Michaela. You don't have a case. But we do."

Richard Kallas looked at her with dead eyes that no amount of plastic surgery could mask.

"Please leave," he said icily, standing up and putting his palms flat on his desk for emphasis.

Ryan looked over at Jessie and shrugged.

"That's your call, Doctor," he said. "But we will be back. And when we return, it'll be with a warrant. Let's go, Jessie."

Ryan headed for the door. She looked back at Kallas, standing there fuming, his hands pressed on his desk and his forearms pulsating in anxiety. She didn't want to go, confident that one more push would make the doctor topple into a pile of his own falsehoods.

"You know we've got you," she said quietly.

Then, despite her reluctance to leave without anything concrete to offer Captain Decker, she followed Ryan. As they reached for the door, Jessie heard an odd click.

"What was that?" she asked as Ryan grabbed the handle.

He tried to turn the knob but it didn't move.

"It's locked," he said, looking for a button or switch on the handle but finding none. He turned around and exasperatedly asked, "What's the deal with the door, Doctor?"

Jessie turned back as well, in time to see Kallas give a sarcastic shrug of his own to go with a nasty smile. She noticed something else too. Behind him on the wall, below the marathon and Iron Man photos, something was amiss with his collection of surgical blades. It took her a moment to realize what the problem was.

One was missing.

Chapter Thirty Three

"You know the most important skill in medicine?" Kallas asked as he held up what looked like a small remote control. "Improvisation."

Then he pushed a button on the remote, casting the office into total darkness.

"Ryan," Jessie called out as she reached for her gun, "he took a knife off his wall. He's armed."

"Got it. Stay quiet," Ryan murmured from somewhere further to her left than he had been moments earlier.

Realizing he must have started moving the second the lights went out, she followed suit, shuffling to the right until she felt her arm brush the wall. As she tried to quiet the pounding rush of blood in her ears, she heard the snap from Ryan unholstering his weapon and she tried to do the same. But her fingers were clumsy and she couldn't seem to get them to work properly.

She wanted to exhale to calm herself but knew that would alert Kallas, who had not made a sound since the lights went out, to her location. The only noise in the office was the soft whir of the air conditioning.

Then she had another idea. On the other side of her belt, she had a small torch flashlight that could be slid out of its holster silently. She managed to extricate it and placed her finger on the "on" button.

But she didn't push yet as two problems became quickly apparent. First, she couldn't warn Ryan about what she was about to do. And second, once she turned on the light, she'd be alerting Kallas to her location. Even if she managed to find him, he might be on her before she could do anything about it.

Any plan she was formulating flew out of her head when she heard the distinct sound of a knee cracking somewhere near Kallas's desk. She ordered herself not to react audibly.

He doesn't know where you are. If you move you might bump into something and expose yourself. Stay still. Stay alert.

Kallas must have realized he'd put himself at risk and stopped moving. Jessie strained her eyes, hoping that might help her adjust to the darkness. But it did no good. The curtains were drawn and the sun had already mostly set so there was no illumination from outside. Kallas, in anticipation of turning off the light, had shut off his computer screen so its glow didn't reveal him. The only thing visible was the green light on the smoke alarm on the ceiling and it offered no help.

A moment later there was another sound, soft and whooshing, that she couldn't identify. It came from somewhere in the middle of the office, less than ten feet from her. As she tried to determine what it was, she slid down the wall in a crouching position. Sensing something close to her, she carefully reached out and her fingertip touched a hard surface. It only took a moment to recall that it was a bookshelf that ran along a section of the wall she was pressed against.

And then it occurred to her. What she'd heard moments earlier was the sound of a large blade being unsheathed from its cover. Kallas was close and he was planning to make a move.

He knows this office better than we do. We have to change the dynamic or he's going to gut us both.

Gripping the torch light, she decided the time had come to do something. She delicately felt around the bookshelf to her right until her fingers found a flat unoccupied spot on the top, about four feet off the floor. She stood up, placed the flashlight in that spot facing the direction where she'd heard Kallas unsheathe the knife, and counted silently to three. Then she pushed the "on" button. The click sounded like a thunderclap.

She took one large step back away from the bookshelf as the torch illuminated the middle of the room. Kallas wasn't in the spotlight but she could hear him moving from somewhere nearby, fast approaching.

A second later, she saw him, advancing on the flashlight, his right arm raised with a long-bladed knife in his hand. Then the light was knocked to the floor as Kallas banged into the bookshelf. She heard the sound of the knife whipping through the air about three feet to her right, swinging wildly as he swiped at what he hoped was her.

The flashlight was now on the floor, facing the other direction, uselessly illuminating the bottom of the bookshelf. Jessie used the chaos to unsnap her holster and pull out her gun. Before she'd even removed it, she heard a deafening, violent thud and a pair of grunts that indicated that Ryan had tried to tackle Kallas.

The murkiness prevented her from doing anything with her gun, as firing it would be a literal shot in the dark. Instead, as she listened to the scrambling, she moved toward the door, feeling around for the light switch. Behind her, there was sickening thwack she couldn't identify, followed by something even more troubling—the return of silence.

If Ryan had gotten the upper hand in the scuffle, he almost certainly would have said something by now. The lack of any noise was a bad sign. Trying to ignore it, she ran her hands all over the wall until she finally felt something. It was the light switch. She flicked it and the room was suddenly bathed in light.

She squinted as she adjusted, looking back in the direction where the fight had occurred as she re-gripped her gun. She took in the scene, processing everything all at once. Lying on the ground unconscious, about six feet from her, was Ryan. Just in front of him was Kallas, who was already leaping up toward her. He must have lost the knife because his hands were empty. She raised her weapon as she flicked off the safety. But before she could fire, he slammed into her, sending the gun flying and smashing her back against the door.

Jessie felt the wind escape her chest as she first collided with the wall and then fell to the ground with Kallas beside her. He appeared stunned. She tried to ignore her suddenly watering eyes and burning chest as she rolled away from the man, who was flailing about, trying to grasp her.

As she gasped for air and tried to regroup, she looked around for her gun. It was nowhere in sight. She glanced over at Ryan. He was breathing but blood was streaming down his forehead. She saw his gun resting underneath his stomach. Just beyond him was the knife.

She crawled in that direction as quickly as she could and was almost to Ryan when she felt a hand grip her ankle. Glancing back, she saw Kallas, now alert and with a nasty smirk on his face. With her free leg, she reared back and kicked, nailing him in the nose.

He yelped loudly but didn't let go. She turned back around, trying to focus on her task. As she clawed at the carpet, Ryan's gun only inches from her fingers, she felt Kallas's other hand grab her calf. A half-second later he yanked back hard, ripping her away from Ryan and back toward him.

As she was pulled back, Jessie looked around desperately for anything to defend herself with. The only thing she saw was the small torch flashlight. It wasn't much but she grabbed it anyway, gripping it tightly in her right hand.

Kallas was on top of her now and grabbed her, twisting her over onto her back. She looked up at him. His nose was bleeding from her kick and it had dripped down onto his formerly perfect white teeth. Still, he smiled malevolently.

"Maybe we should make our own video, Jessie," he snarled as he pinned her hips down with his hands and knees. "The one with Missy was good. But I think I could poke a few more holes in you."

"You recorded yourself killing her?" Jessie asked, in stunned disbelief.

"It was her best film yet," he said excitedly. "I put graphics on it and everything. It's titled *Playing Doctor*. Funny, huh? I bet I could come up with an even better one for you."

He chuckled. Jessie knew that this moment, when he was enthralled with his own cleverness, might be her last chance to surprise him before he focused in on what he planned to do to her. So she took advantage of it.

Jessie swung the torch flashlight at him, aiming for his right eye. She knew she'd made a direct hit when she made contact with something softer than bone. The sudden scream that escaped his lips reinforced her certainty.

He reached up to stop her but she pulled the light back and swung again, not taking aim this time. She managed to smash the thing against his teeth before the force of the blow sent it back into his open mouth, causing him to gag.

Kallas shook his head wildly and she lost her grip on the light. He reached up and tore it from his throat. As he looked down at her with his one good eye, the fury and hatred he felt was palpable.

He slapped her hard across the face with his left hand, as he grabbed a handful of her hair with his right. She tried to bat his arms away but he was too strong. He lifted her head up by the hair and slammed her head back down on the thin carpet, making her skull rattle and her vision blur. She felt him lift her head again. But this time she couldn't find the strength to swat at him. She clenched her eyes tight in anticipation of what was coming.

He was just about to slam her down again when Jessie heard an earsplitting crunch. A moment later, the weight of Kallas's body was no longer on top of her. Despite the pain, she opened her eyes and tried to focus them.

To her right, Dr. Richard Kallas was lying on his stomach. Two uniformed LAPD officers had him pinned down as one of them cuffed his hands behind his back. Kallas was still howling in pain and rage.

But after a moment, his screams began to sound more distant. In the seconds before it happened, Jessie realized she was losing consciousness. And then everything went dark.

CHAPTER THIRTY FOUR

Jessie wasn't out for long.

When she came to, she was lying on the exam table in the room where she'd been moved to. According to Captain Decker, who was standing over her with a worried expression, she'd only been out for about ninety seconds.

"How's Hernandez?" she asked, ignoring her aching jaw.

"They're checking him out now in the office. He's conscious but woozy. The EMT said the cut on his head isn't that deep. How are you?"

"Sore."

"Yeah, well, it's a good thing you texted me the exact address and suite number of this office or we'd still be looking for you and your head would be split open like a melon."

Jessie tried to sit up but felt mildly nauseated and lay back down. She took a deep breath and when she was sure she could speak, she replied.

"What's the deal with Kallas?"

"The doctor with the disturbing cutlery collection? He's being transported to Cedars-Sinai to get that eye looked at. You really did a number on him. I'm assuming he's your top suspect in the Penn murder and that's why you brazenly disobeyed direct orders."

"He claims to have a video of the killing," Jessie said, trying not to rub it in. "We should get people on that ASAP. And that's not the only reason I disobeyed orders, Captain."

"I'm all ears," he replied with raise eyebrows.

For half a second, Jessie debated whether to confide in him. But ultimately, if she wanted to keep herself and the people she cared about safe, she had no choice.

"I need you to shut the door for this," she said quietly.

Decker looked more surprised than she'd ever seen him. But without another word, he walked over and closed the door.

She sighed deeply, and then began.

Jessie pretended her head wasn't splitting in half.

She popped another ibuprofen as she watched Richard Kallas through a two-way mirror in the observation room. He sat cuffed to a bolted-down metal table in a Central Station interrogation room. His left eye was bandaged, though the doctor had said it would eventually heal. He was missing a tooth but nothing had been done about that yet.

It had been three hours since the attack at Kallas's office and the world seemed very different now, though still not as safe as Jessie hoped. Since she didn't know when she'd be free, she had called Kat Gentry, who had just returned from enjoying a multi-day date with Deputy Mitch Connor, the Lake Arrowhead liaison for the San Bernardino Sheriff's Department.

She asked if Kat could relieve Garland Moses on the Hannah-watching front. But Garland instead offered to let her crash at his place. Jessie didn't mind, as the more people she trusted around Hannah, the better.

Ryan was still at the hospital. Doctors were confident he could be released soon but wanted to keep him overnight as a precaution. They'd wanted her to stay too but she insisted on discharging herself to conduct this interrogation. She promised that she would return afterward and spend the night there so they could keep her under observation.

The Butters situation still weighed heavily on her mind. She wanted to talk to Kallas with a clear head but wasn't sure she could until she got an update on that situation. As if on cue, Captain Decker stepped into the observation room and asked the camera tech to step out for a moment.

"What have you got for me?" she asked him hopefully.

"I can't get into specifics," he said quietly. "But it's happening as we speak. We'll know more by tomorrow."

"That's it?"

"That's all I can share at this point," he insisted. "The less you know right now, the better for you. Just trust that people are taking it seriously. You just focus on Kallas right now."

"You sure I'm authorized to conduct this investigation? No one's going to drag me out on a disciplinary charge in the middle of it?"

She knew it was a cheap shot but she'd held her tongue for this long and just couldn't contain herself any longer.

"Don't push it, Hunt," he warned, though not unkindly. "Department policy requires that a detective be involved in any formal interrogation, so Trembley will be in there with you. But he knows that you'll be taking the lead and won't step on your toes."

"Thanks, Captain," she said as they left the room and stood outside the interrogation room door."

"No problem," he said. "Just remember, I'll be watching. So please don't stab him in the other eye."

"I'll try my hardest," she assured him as she opened the door and stepped inside.

Detective Alan Trembley was already in there, as was one uniformed officer. Trembley smiled at her knowingly, oblivious to his own unkempt curly blond hair and the glasses halfway down the bridge of his nose. In addition to being boring, the guy was a bit scattered. But he'd come a long way since she'd first met him. More importantly right now, she knew he wouldn't get in the way of what she needed to do.

She looked over at Kallas, who was staring at her dully.

"Is he medicated?" she asked Trembley.

"He is," Kallas said before Trembley could reply. "But don't let that stop you from attempting to outwit him. But before you try, I wanted to ask: how's your detective buddy doing? No brain damage, I hope?"

Jessie smiled at him. Something about the guy's smarm seemed pathetic when he wasn't in his medical tower office.

"No new damage," she told him. "He's alert and remembers your attempt to murder him, if that's what you're wondering."

"I was purely concerned for his welfare," Kallas said. "I want him to be in tip-top shape when I sue him for police misconduct for attacking me without warning in my place of business."

Jessie leaned in and spoke slowly, relishing every word.

"Good luck with that. Oh, by the way, I just thought you should know—we have video from your office building showing Michaela leaving on three separate occasions, long after business hours."

Kallas didn't seem fazed.

"That doesn't mean anything," Kallas insisted. "I agreed to see her at that time because she was worried about being recognized."

Jessie nodded sympathetically.

"I see," she said. "We also found video of a man in a hoodie driving your car about six blocks from Michaela's place on the night of the murder."

Kallas nodded expectantly.

"I've been meaning to file a police report about that. I think my car was stolen and taken for a joyride that night. I parked it on the street and when I found it the next morning, it was in a different spot and missing gas."

He smiled as he said it, not even trying to sound convincing. Something about his brazen willingness to lie when the truth was obvious felt strangely familiar.

"How unfortunate that you didn't file that report then," Jessie noted.

"Here's the thing, Jessie," he said, leaning in himself now. "If you really had anything on me, you wouldn't be in here right now trying to work me. This is a sign of your sad desperation. My attorney is going to have a field day with you."

Jessie leaned back in her chair and studied him, wondering how he was able to compartmentalize the different parts of himself: the man in front of her now and the creature who had committed that vile act two nights earlier.

"I'm not desperate, Dick," she said softly. "I just wanted to give you a chance to tell me how you did it in your own words. It will likely be your last chance. Once your lawyer gets here, you won't have the chance. And I know you're dying to."

"This is the best you've got?" he asked haughtily, though his one working eye betrayed some apprehension. "You're trying to bait me into some kind of false confession?"

"We found the video, Dick."

"What?"

"The video of you assaulting and stabbing Michaela to death, we found it. Thanks for letting me know it existed. We might never have thought to look for something so depraved on our own. But because of your tip, we looked, and we found it in that innocuous-sounding computer file you titled 'graft analysis.' As you know, it's definitive. You'll be convicted. It'll probably take the length of a sitcom episode for the jury to complete their deliberations."

Kallas stared at her silently. She could tell from his expression that he knew she was telling the truth. She continued.

"So like I said, the only reason I'm in here is to let you give me your version. I don't need it. We've got you. It's not like a confession will make much difference. They can't execute you twice, after all. But as you know, I'm a profiler so I'm inherently curious about this kind of aberrant behavior. So I'm giving you one last chance to come clean. If you're not interested, that's your call. I'll head out for a late dinner. Just know that once I walk out that door, you'll have lost the last sympathetic audience you'll ever get."

She stood up. He said nothing.

"Tick-tock, Dick," she said as she headed for the door.

She was just grabbing the handle when she heard him speak.

"Wait."

If they hadn't sedated her, she wouldn't have slept at all that night.

Kallas's words echoed in her mind all the way to the hospital after the interrogation and resumed again the moment she got up. She replayed them once more as she stood in the shower, letting the warm water massage the twisted muscles in her back.

He had gone through every detail of the crime meticulously, from the moment he'd decided to kill Michaela until he drove off afterward. His description of the murder matched the video he'd taken perfectly.

But it wasn't the actual killing that made it hard to get the case out of her head. It was Kallas's demeanor. She still recalled his answer when she asked why he'd killed her.

"You don't get it," he'd said as he sat in the interrogation room, his body still coiled in excitement at recalling what he'd done. "I'd seen her movies. I could tell from the bored look in her eyes that she needed something more. So I sought her out. And I found her. We found each other. And it was better than I could have imagined. One time she wore a nurse's uniform. The next she pretended to be a patient. We used almost every room in the office. It was a delight."

"So what changed?" Jessie asked him.

"She lied to me."

"What did she lie about?" Jessie had asked, working hard to keep judgment out of her voice.

"I told her that I would take care of her, that she should stop having dates with those pathetic fans. I also told her that after she'd completed whatever movies she was contracted to do, she should stop shooting them entirely. I would make up her lost income. She said she would make the changes. But she didn't stop."

"She still saw other clients?" Jessie prodded.

"Several. I confronted her about it and she acted as if she thought I was kidding. She said I couldn't possibly be serious. When I told her that I was, she said I was weirding her out and that we couldn't see each other anymore. That wasn't right. So I made things right."

"Richard," Jessie asked, knowing it would probably be her last question, "looking back, do you feel guilty at all for what you did?"

"For what exactly?" he replied, genuinely perplexed.

"For raping and killing a seventeen-year-old girl, for stabbing her nine times, for ending the life of another person just because she wouldn't be exactly what you wanted her to be? I almost understand losing yourself in the moment. But afterward, in the days since, have you felt bad at all?"

She pictured Hannah lying on that bed instead of Michaela. The two of them were so alike—troubled, smart girls, damaged by the world but still with promising futures.

Kallas looked at her like she was speaking a foreign language.

"Jessie," he said slowly, as if he was talking to a child, "she lied to *me*. She wronged *me*. She ruined the plans I'd made for us. Why should I feel bad for something *she* did? Ask her if she felt bad."

"I can't," Jessie reminded him. "She's dead."

She turned off the shower, unsure how long she'd been standing there reliving their conversation in her mind. As she wrapped a towel around herself and stepped out, her brain continued to circle around some truth that she couldn't quite pinpoint. It was right there, at the edge of her consciousness, teasing her.

She closed the shower door and as it clicked shut, something in her mind clicked too. She realized what had been bothering her, the itch she couldn't quite scratch. She had been imagining Hannah in Michaela's position, a potential victim of a horrible crime.

But the more she thought about it, the more Hannah reminded her of someone else. The bold, pointless lies told so easily, the utter disregard for anyone's well-being besides her own, the seeming lack of empathy for those around her.

Hannah reminded Jessie more of Richard Kallas than of Michaela Penn. And though she'd just spent ten minutes in a hot shower, Jessie suddenly felt horribly cold.

CHAPTER THIRTY FIVE

For a criminal profiler, Jessie Hunt felt pretty stupid.

She hadn't figured it out when Ryan insisted on driving them back downtown after being discharged from the hospital. She hadn't figured it out when he suggested they use their much deserved forced day off after tangling with a murderer to go bowling at the Lucky Strike at L.A. Live in the middle of the afternoon. She hadn't even figured it out when she walked into the place and saw balloons and streamers.

It wasn't until everyone jumped out to yell "Happy Birthday" that she realized what was going on. To be honest, she had completely forgotten that today was her thirtieth birthday. But apparently Ryan hadn't.

How he'd managed to coordinate all this while in the middle of two investigations, courtroom testimony, and a hospital-requiring run-in with a sociopathic killer was beyond her. She looked over at him and was amused by his Cheshire cat smile.

"You're sneaky," she said playfully. "You said I needed to clear Thursday evening."

He shrugged nonchalantly as if it was no big deal. Before he could say anything, they were swarmed by people. Hannah was there, with Garland, Kat, and a guy Jessie didn't recognize but assumed was Deputy Mitch Connor.

Dr. Lemmon stood nearby as did Agent Jack Dolan and Patrick "Murph" Murphy, the federal marshal who'd protected her when her father was stalking her. Detectives Trembley and Callum Reid and officers Beatty and Nettles from Central Station were in attendance, as was Ryan's ample-gutted buddy from Westside division, Detective Brady Bowen. Even Captain Decker had showed up.

They all hugged her gingerly, aware that she had been hospitalized recently.

"Hey, at least you got out fast this time," Kat said drily. "I'm used to you convalescing in hospital beds for weeks at a time."

"Me too," Jessie said. "Thanks for stopping by to watch Hannah last night. I hope it didn't mess up anything with that mountain man deputy over there."

"Nah. Mitch and I needed a little break to come up for air, if you know what I mean," she said, winking obviously.

"I do know what you mean, Katherine. But thanks for leaving little to the imagination. Just try to keep your clothes on until the party's over, okay?"

"I'm not making any promises," he friend said, already returning to the lane where Mitch was waiting for her.

When she walked off, Hannah came over, looking more tentative than usual.

"How are you doin', big sis?" she asked, using that term for the first time.

"I'm getting by," Jessie told her. "Sorry for abandoning you to the care of relative strangers for the night."

"That's okay. Until a few months ago, you were a relative stranger. Besides, Kat and the snarky geriatric are both way cooler than you. So it worked out."

Her wry smile indicated that she was mostly kidding.

"You didn't ruin any of Garland's doilies, I hope?" Jessie asked.

"Nope—didn't even see any. He must have hidden them somewhere to keep my grubby fingers off them."

"Smart move," Jessie noted.

"Perhaps," Hannah conceded. "But what he doesn't know is that however much money he saved by hiding his home valuables from me, he's about to lose in bowling. We just made a friendly wager. And I don't know if you're aware of this, but before my life went to hell, I was in the bowling club at school. And I was good."

"Seriously?"

"Yep. I'm about to clean him out after I have a little cake. Don't warn him."

"I won't," Jessie promised, crossing her heart.

She watched Hannah head over to the cake table and felt an unusual sense of relief. Bowling parties, cake, and casual, pleasant interactions were at such a premium she wanted to savor the moment. When there was finally a lull in the well wishes, Captain Decker came over.

"It looks like half of Central Station is here, Captain," Jessie noted. "Who's going to solve all the crimes and stuff?"

"Actually, I'm about to announce that they all have to get back in a minute. But I figured the bad guys would give us a thirty-minute break. They do that, right?" he said, smiling sardonically.

"Well, thanks for coming, even if only briefly," she said.

"I would have stopped by regardless, Hunt. I wanted to give you an update on things. I figured you wouldn't mind, even at your party."

"You figured right," Jessie told him. "What's going on?"

"First of all, what I couldn't tell you last night was that after our little chat at the doctor's office, I went directly to headquarters to talk to Chief Laird. I insisted on the immediate revocation of your suspensions and any disciplinary actions. He caved on that pretty quickly. Then I addressed your concerns about Commander Butters and Valley Bureau. It turns out that Internal Affairs was already conducting a months-long investigation of both. That's part of why you were waved off. They didn't want you interfering and screwing up a potential case."

"How aggressively could they have been investigating if this stuff was going on in nearly plain sight?" Jessie demanded.

"A fair question—one I broached with him. He didn't have great answer for me. But after I brought all of your allegations to his attention, he immediately called in the I.A. team and put the wood to them. In the approximately sixteen hours since our meeting, several things have happened."

"Should I be sitting down for this?" Jessie asked.

"Maybe," he replied. "First, Laird got court orders to immediately expand the use of the wires already up on several officers. He rightly suspected that there would be a lot of chatter in the wake of Kallas's arrest. Investigators checked the footage from the Travelodge where you alleged Butters met with Michaela Penn."

"And?"

"We have matches on the dates where her GPS phone data shows her there. We see him arriving, opening the motel room door when she arrives, and leaving separately hours later. There are also cash withdrawals earlier on each of those days that correspond with the rate she quoted on that agency's website. In addition, your FBI agent friend, Dolan, is having the cash in Michaela's envelope tested for fingerprints. It's a long shot but if even one bill has his prints on it, it could be dispositive. And there's more."

"Please don't let me stop you," Jessie insisted, trying not to sound giddy.

"They found an unmarked car in the Van Nuys Station motor pool with paint scratches that match Hernandez's car. They also have conversations on those surveillance wire recordings between Butters and Costabile, as well as between Costabile and multiple Valley Bureau officers, that will be hard to explain in court."

"What kind of conversations?" Jessie asked.

"Without getting too specific, I'll just say there were references to rushed cremations, and hiding evidence, as well as past and future threats and attacks against people who were 'getting in the way.'"

"That's pretty specific, Captain."

"I may have said too much," Decker replied, smiling. "In any case, it's my understanding that a massive sweep arresting over a dozen cops, including at least eight in Valley Bureau, will be happening in about . . . what time is it now?"

"It's one thirty-eight," Jessie told him.

"In about twenty-two minutes, which is another reason we have to go. Some of our people will be assisting."

"I'd be happy to help," Jessie said, unable to hide the glee she felt.

"That's okay, Hunt. I don't want you anywhere nearby when this goes down. You should focus on eating cake and throwing that heavy ball down a long hunk of wood for the next little bit. We've got this."

"Yes, sir," Jessie replied.

Decker started to turn to leave but then seemed to remember something.

"One last thing," he added. "Detective Parker in Vice wanted me to let you know that Filthy Films is being temporarily shut down."

"Only temporarily?" she asked, aghast.

"I'm afraid so," he said. "They're investigating but she doesn't think they're going to be able to prove anyone knew Michaela Penn was underage. They did the minimum required to check her identity. I think we can both reasonably surmise that they knew her info was bogus. But proving that will be difficult. However, all of the Missy Mack films are being pulled from their site."

"That won't stop people from seeing them," Jessie said. "Those movies will still be all over the aggregator sites. They may even become more popular because they'll be extra taboo now."

"You're probably right," Decker conceded. "But we've done all we can on our end."

"So we move on and footage of a seventeen-year-old dead girl having sex continues to circulate on the internet?"

Decker sighed. It was clear that he didn't have any good answer for that.

"Happy birthday, Hunt. I'm really glad you're alive to celebrate it," he said. Before she could respond, he turned and yelled to the bowling alley generally. "All on-duty personnel, it's time to go. We have a pressing assignment."

As the Central Station folks unhappily filed out, Garland Moses walked over.

"You don't have to go too?" she asked.

"Me? No. I'm about to sweep the floor with your sister in bowling. Besides, my days of personally arresting multiple corrupt cops are well in the past, Ms. Hunt."

Jessie shook her head in disbelief.

"You already know about that? How do you get access to everything so fast? It's almost like..."

She stopped suddenly, her mind racing.

"Almost like what?" he asked curiously.

"It's almost like you have inside information that, if you wanted to, you could share with trusted law enforcement personnel in the hope that they could correct miscarriages of justice before they got swept under the rug."

"That is quite a lot and oddly specific, Ms. Hunt," Garland replied with an inscrutable smile.

"Yeah," she agreed. "I guess I'm a real Chatty Cathy."

"If you say so," he said noncommittally.

"Speaking of chatty folks," she said, deciding to let him off the hook for now. "How did it go with Hannah last night? Are you two besties now?"

Garland's smile faded and she saw immediately that something was wrong. All her fears from before, the connections she'd made between Hannah and Richard Kallas, resurfaced.

"What?" she asked.

"Let's save it for another time," he suggested.

"No. What is it? You profiled her, didn't you, like I asked?"

"I had a pleasant conversation with her," he answered calmly.

"Then why is there a massive pit in my stomach right now?"

"Listen, Jessie," he said, using her first name for what she suspected was the first time ever. "We can discuss this in greater detail at a more appropriate time. For now, just know that you don't need to overreact. Hannah and I spoke a fair bit and most of our time together was quite agreeable."

She was about to press him on what "most" of their time together meant when her phone rang. She didn't recognize the number but something made her answer anyway.

"Hello," she said.

There was a moment of silence before anyone spoke. The delay reminded her of the full second before she got the call threatening Hannah. Sure enough, when a voice finally began to speak, it was digitally altered.

"You should have quit when you had the chance, little lass. I may pay a price now. But one day, maybe sooner than you think, you will. I hope it was worth it."

Then the call ended. Though there was no way to prove it, she knew who had made the call. She could only recall one person ever referring to her as "little lass." It had happened just the other day, when she bumped into a cop in a police station hallway and, with no one else nearby, he'd threatened her.

The call had come from Sergeant Hank Costabile.

Now she had a new enemy.

Now Available for Pre-Order!

THE PERFECT ALIBI
(A Jessie Hunt Psychological Suspense Thriller—Book Eight)

"A masterpiece of thriller and mystery. Blake Pierce did a magnificent job developing characters with a psychological side so well described that we feel inside their minds, follow their fears and cheer for their success. Full of twists, this book will keep you awake until the turn of the last page."

—Books and Movie Reviews, Roberto Mattos (re *Once Gone*)

THE PERFECT ALIBI is book #8 in a new psychological suspense series by bestselling author Blake Pierce, which begins with *The Perfect Wife*, a #1 bestseller (and free download) with nearly 500 five-star reviews.

A suburban wife and mom escapes from the grasp of a psychotic serial killer—only to wind up murdered weeks later.

Was it a coincidence?

Or is there a serial killer out there playing a sick game of catch and release–and catch again?

Can famed FBI agent Jessie Hunt, 29, shake off her personal trauma and enter this killer's mind? Can she save the next victim–and maybe even herself–before it is too late?

A fast-paced psychological suspense thriller with unforgettable characters and heart-pounding suspense, THE PERFECT ALIBI is book #8 in a riveting new series that will leave you turning pages late into the night.

Book #9 in the Jessie Hunt series—THE PERFECT NEIGHBOR—is now also available.

THE PERFECT ALIBI
(A Jessie Hunt Psychological Suspense Thriller–Book Eight)

Did you know that I've written multiple novels in the mystery genre? If you haven't read all my series, click the image below to download a series starter!

Printed in Great Britain
by Amazon

72646402R00118